TO THE EDGE OF THE SEA

For Lucille
Happy writing
& singing
& improvising —
to all yes's!
[signature]

To the Edge of the Sea

⚓

[signature]

Anne McDonald

thistledown press

Thistledown Press Ltd.
118 - 20th Street West
Saskatoon, Saskatchewan, S7M 0W6
www.thistledownpress.com

Library and Archives Canada Cataloguing in Publication

McDonald, Anne, 1960-
To the edge of the sea / Anne McDonald.
ISBN 978-1-897235-85-0

I. Title.
PS8625.D62475T67 2011   C813'.6   C2011-901710-5

Author photo by Don Hall
Cover and book design by Jackie Forrie
Printed and bound in Canada

Thistledown Press gratefully acknowledges the financial assistance of the Canada Council for the Arts, the Saskatchewan Arts Board, and the Government of Canada through the Canada Book Fund for its publishing program.

Acknowledgements

I am grateful to all those who have given their encouragement and support, and shared their stories with me. I wish to thank the Saskatchewan Arts Board for funding given to me to write early drafts of this novel. Excerpts of this work have appeared in *the society*, and on CBC radio. The manuscript was awarded First Alternate for the Hicks Award and The Saskatchewan Writers Guild's Writers and Artists Colonies at St. Peter's Abbey have been instrumental in providing time, peace, and inspiration for this writing. In particular I am thankful for their hospitality on our storm-stayed night when the ending of this novel finally came.

Many thanks to my writing colleagues and teachers who have looked at early drafts of this work — Brian Miller, Shelley Banks, Seema Goel, Stefan Riches, Olive Senior, David Carpenter at the Sage Hill Writing Experience, Sarah Sheard, and especially Francie Greenslade and my sister Mary McDonald. Also much thanks to the writers and artists who have attended the St. Pete's Writing Colonies over the years.

I am grateful to my family for their love and encouragement. Much thanks goes to my sisters Margaret, Mary and Sharon who have been there all along the way and to my brothers-in-law for their barbeque dinners, and their knowledge of fish and Niagara Falls. My niece Megan and nephew John who have grown up during the writing of this book have reminded me of what it is like to be the ages of the characters in this novel, have prodded me with questions of when it would be done, and helped me think about questions of belief in oneself. My mother's optimism and faith know no bounds.

I wish also to thank David Sealy for his unending encouragement, love, and inspiration, and for everything he does both for me and our writing lives.

Thanks to Al Forrie and Jackie Forrie at Thistledown Press for their belief in this novel and creating such a wonderful book.

Thank you is not enough to John Lent for his great generosity in sharing his knowledge and his guidance on so many levels. His eye for detail and imagery and his ear for the music of language have made the shaping and balancing of this book so much more than it was. His sense of humour, gracious patience, and honesty have been so wonderful for a first time author. I can't say enough.

Although I have used real people and events in this book I have freely fictionalized intents and events, dates and situations, and all should be read as fiction.

For my mother and father who gave me childhood summers at the beach in Prince Edward Island and for Mae Gus McDonald, Frances Griffith, Skip McDonald and all those who told me stories of their childhood and of my father's.

Always for David.

PROLOGUE

ALEX STANDS WAIST-DEEP IN THE WATER, HIS hair falling heavily over his forehead, gray green sea encircling him. His shadow plays tricks in the light in the sea, his lock of hair looking as if it is a fish.

Just like the fish he'd watched the day before from his father's boat. They should have been finished their day's catch and heading for home. But the day had been hot, too still, and no one had caught anything. Their boat was empty, listless as the day.

He'd been jigging carelessly when he'd seen the small cod. The fish hung suspended in the green sea. Alex stopped making even small movements with his line. He didn't want to catch it even if it was the only fish they caught that day. Better to be clean with none than sullied by one lone fish.

The fish stayed beside the boat, getting no closer to Alex's line, seeming to invite Alex to join it in the green sun water. Alex reached out as if he could touch the fish and it moved away from him, away from the boat and lines, its tail moving slightly, taking its leave as if it barely noticed the leaving.

Now Alex is walking in, intending to go over his head. In order to swim he will have to go where he can't touch bottom and will have to rise, float. The water tugs lightly on his bare body, pushes against him and pulls away again. His fish hair shadow keeps him company on his walk out, keeps him safe, and there is his older brother on shore, watchman. Then Alex is in over his head, his eyes open while the ceiling of water falls away from him.

Reggie sees his brother sink and disappear, not a hand raised, nothing to be seen at all in the darkness of the sea. Reggie is five feet up from the water, on the tide-flattened sand, with no height to see better. He counts to ten, but at six he can't wait any longer. He looks around for help. There is no one else. They are alone. No one lives down here right by the shore. Foolish. The wind, the storms, the water too close.

Reggie runs down to the water's edge. He can't swim. He can't tell where Alex is anymore in this sea of sea. It all looks the same, no points of land, no way to mark this landscape. He is helpless, frozen on the shore. Foolish, both of them foolish.

Alex closes his mouth just in time. The beauty of the water overhead startles him, bubbles of green light caught between the sea and the sun rise and fall with the water's slight wave. He sinks farther down; the water rises above him, suspends itself over him.

Reggie kicks off his shoes. He will have to go in. The salt and water cling heavily to his pants. The water sucks at him, threatens to topple him, sucking and pulling. He goes in deeper, past his waist, up to his chest. He doesn't realize he is crying. Thinks it is the sea he tastes. He calls out, barely a whisper, not hearing it himself — "Alex."

The water weighs on Alex, tries to hold him down. He opens his mouth and it fills with water, with salt that chokes him. He is afraid and he kicks his legs, moves his arms, and he rises, knows even in his panic that he has swum. Knows now too he is as free as the cod, owner of the sea. Both possessor and possessed.

Reggie stops and tries to hold himself as still as possible, his arms clenched, held tight at his side, a post in the sea, the water up to his neck. Alex is there in front of him, deeper than Reggie can touch. He begins to move backwards, keeps his back to the shore and his eyes on the sea and Alex. It's safer that way. Never turn your back on something you can't trust.

Alex follows his brother, stops when his toes feel the rippled sand of the shallow water where he can touch bottom and stand. "Lay out your clothes to dry, Reg, and come back in. I'll show you. I just didn't do it right the first time." With a laugh, trying to get his brother to see, Alex says, "If we ever fall in we can save each other."

Reggie, who has reached the shore, starts taking off his clothes. He walks up to the top of the beach and lays them flat over the dune grass. Then he lies down in the sand and crosses his arms under his head. His fear has settled into the pit of his stomach, broken down into a blanket of dirt, grit that can be stirred up, clouding his insides, making him murky with fear at the slightest movement. He closes his eyes and dreams of fields blowing with hay, flowering with potatoes, the wind in the sea the wind through the fields. Tilling a field, in a line straight down, and the turn at the end like the sway of a girl's hip. But he can't get the sea out of his mind. The sway of the field turns into a wave and then all the straight tilled lines move with the wind, rise left, then right, up and down till it too becomes a field of sea.

Alex, his hands still in fists, stays in the water. He walks back out, testing the depth slowly. He can float in water as deep as his chest now, facing in to the shore. He wishes Reggie would come and join him. They could have such a good time together. It is lonely being the only one.

ONE

"What child, if the future could be revealed to it in infancy, would not shrink from the dangers and burdens even of the most prosperous and heroic life?"
— *London Daily News*, 1862-1863.
Goldwin Smith letters referring to Canada

"Our colonies are rather too fond of us, and embrace us, if anything, too closely."
— *London Times*, October 24th, 1864

June 17th, 1864. Quebec City Legislature

JOHN A. MACDONALD WATCHED GEORGE BROWN WAVE his arms about, blustering on. What a fool. He'd rather be a drunk. A man who drank was practical. He knew what came before and what was needed next. He was good at creating the future, admittedly because he always needed to make sure of it, needed to know where the next drink would be. Brown would be better if he indulged. A man could work with him then, could count on a generosity of spirit, good will, like Cartier, or McGee. Macdonald looked over at them, nodded at Cartier who was watching him. Macdonald shrugged. There was nothing to do but wait now, everyone was waiting. There was a certain ease about a man who drank, unhindered by convictions. What a man wouldn't do for his convictions — blind sense. He sighed and turned away. But here it was; he needed Brown. If he and Cartier agreed to consider a federal union, Brown and his party would support them and the country could move on.

He looked out the window. Summer quick and hot had suddenly arrived after a late spring. The leaves of the sumacs along the river were just now beginning to uncurl against their furred trunks. Not like home, not like his lake in Kingston.

There the grasses by the lake would be growing long and wild, the flowers beginning to start and the birds in full song. Macdonald raised his hand to his forehead. He was hot; beads of sweat formed along his brow. Even the breeze was slight and slow waiting for Brown to finish. Winter flies droned in the corner of the window. Macdonald knew what was coming; everyone did. For God's sake would Brown just get on with it, do it, it was so hot. He wiped his forehead again, shifted in his seat.

Macdonald wondered if he could do the same — support Brown's party, change face, change allegiance, all in order to get the one thing he wanted, like Brown was willing to do. Though he was so slow in doing it, Macdonald was beginning to doubt Brown. Maybe Brown still hoped against hope that he could form the government; maybe he'd become unwilling to support Macdonald and Cartier and then they wouldn't be able to form government either. The country still in a stalemate. No one able to lead. Macdonald looked back at Brown who was turning red as he spoke. He knew he never would be — for better or worse — he'd never be a man like Brown. Better, far better, he thought, he and his follies. Who didn't love a man with follies? The people proved it over and over again. And Brown hated him for it — but what did he expect? Didn't he understand the game? No. And that was the problem. They all depended on a man who didn't even realize there was a game. All of them waiting for the impossible man to make things possible.

The Canadas continually faltered, and the government fell. Four governments in two years, the country hobbled, unable to go one step forward without falling back. Canada east, west, upper, lower — too equal. A curse for a country. Like brothers with no parent to give direction, they'd always fight, always one trying to have more than the other. It would go on endlessly. Macdonald sighed. A continual dance is what it had been, the partners circling round each other, one pulling the other too hard, or not hard enough. And him caught in the middle.

Brown called out how John A's and Cartier's government had fallen, again, less than two months in office. Macdonald laughed a soft laugh. Brown couldn't resist, even though no one else could do better, and certainly not Brown who'd gotten into office for one day only, till he, Macdonald, had double-shuffled him out. Brown was a dupe, gullible. Macdonald shook his head and shrugged his shoulders. He'd been mired in the muck of Canadian politics for the past twenty years, and now here it was, Brown, the inane, the ridiculous, the only way out.

A wind blew in through the window, lifted a few papers from a desk. Macdonald watched them float lazily through the air and slowly drift to the floor. No one leaned forward to pick them up as Brown paused and turned directly towards him. Macdonald pushed back his shoulders, sat up straight. Made his face look attentive.

"We can not continue in this way," Brown called. Macdonald watched as Brown raised his arm, saw the men of the house turn so as to see them both. Macdonald rose, waited. He shifted on his feet, thought of how he would sound, his voice calm, powerful. He knew how the men would turn to watch him and listen. Brown looked at him, said nothing. Macdonald smiled, clasped his hands behind his back. He saw one of the papers on the floor lift slightly and sink back down. Still Brown didn't speak, but just stood there with his hand opened out towards him.

Stymied, Brown wasn't going to be able to do it, Macdonald thought. It'd be up to him to do Brown's work for him. Macdonald started to open his mouth, was about to make a joke, when he looked at Brown.

Brown stared at Macdonald. He wanted here and now, respect, public acknowledgement from Macdonald that he, Brown, was the only one able to and willing to make their government possible. He stared at Macdonald, forcing him to be silent, to meet his gaze, to publicly admit that he, George Brown was the answer.

Macdonald paused. He glanced away a moment and back at Brown. The men of the house were silent. Macdonald met Brown's gaze and slowly nodded his head. Yes. They all needed Brown. He needed Brown. Silly to let the man's ridiculousness stop him. Yes, he stood silent, nodded again. He waited for Brown to speak and did not smile.

Brown waited another moment. He looked out at the men. His chest swelled with his breath. He had what he wanted. He smiled. Everyone knew, everyone saw. Macdonald could not outdo him. Macdonald needed him and all knew it. He spoke loudly and clearly, "I, my party and I, will support . . . " Brown paused as he uttered each word, "this government;" he waved his arm towards Macdonald and Cartier who stood then too. Brown, Macdonald, and Cartier were the only men standing in the hall. The others leaned forward, all of them silent, attentive to Brown. "if, union, a federal union. A confederation, in fact, of all of the provinces of British North America . . . "

Macdonald sighed. Still such bluster, such self-importance, Brown was missing the momentum, the moment dissipating in the heat, and the drift of wind.

" . . . is sought."

Brown's ending was abrupt and Macdonald, who had looked away, looked startled as they all turned towards him.

Brown gazed at Macdonald. It was Macdonald's turn. Brown had done his bit, and the country would remember him. His wife Anne had said it that morning. He, George Brown, was the bigger man, the country would know. And Macdonald knew too — he had to respect Brown now. Brown smiled, swelled more. He was the one the country would remember. What choice did Macdonald have? He would accept Brown's offer. A wind had begun to stir and Brown felt a slight chill in his damp clothes, and shivered in the heat.

Macdonald regarded the men of the house. Everyone was silent. It seemed to him that everybody held their breath, that time itself had paused, and now waited for him to speak. The possibility of change beginning to occur to them all. Macdonald lifted his hand towards Brown. In a loud voice he began. "We accept the . . . "

The rest of his words drowned out by cheering and hands pounding desks by the men who'd been waiting, the country waiting, everything and everyone holding still so long and suddenly let loose, swept under by the tide of the future washing over them. Macdonald stopped. He stood silent, his mouth open, overwhelmed by the noise of the men surrounding him.

The sound became a rhythmic pounding that echoed round the room, out the open window, travelled south to the border, and down and out the St. Lawrence River where it passed a red island sitting calm in the afternoon of a June sun. It reverberated across the ocean to the far shore where men in London walking home from late dinner parties heard a slapping sound behind them as though the sea licked at their heels, making them stumble. They turned, and seeing nothing, shook their heads. It was only their imaginations, nothing. Ignoring the sea sound of change as the noise continued, the men of the legislature chanting Macdonald's and Brown's names till they rose from their seats and crossed the floor to each other. Macdonald and Brown stood there beside each other, shrunk by the sound engulfing them as they both looked out in wonder.

Tuesday, August 30th, 1864. Charlottetown

THE CIRCUS TENT ROSE IN TOWN WARM with red dust and a faltering sea breeze. A group of boys hung about hoping to help, hoping to see the show. Alex, alone inside the tent, looked up as the tent high above him billowed in and out and up. The sound of it as it moved with the wind, like the sound of the water as it slapped against the hull of their boat. He held his breath as the sides of the tent rolled down vast around him, enclosing him.

The men outside grabbed the lines, staked the tent down. The boys helped and the men hammered in the spikes, attaching the material to the ground. Alex heard them distant, his breath in time to the flutter of the walls with the wind. He looked up again. Wanted to reach his arms out to touch the red suspended above him, like a child believing it can touch the sky.

In his dreams he had not imagined the size and sound of it. How it would spread out large around him, breathing, moving with the swell of the air. The tall centre pole pierced the sky through. As if the tent were anchored to the sky, not the earth.

Or was the sky itself held by the tent? Tent and sky together shifting in the breeze.

Two men came in on the far side and Alex went to push his way out under the flap of the tent. He turned back as he got to the red wall. The peace of it there, the wind stilled and the warmth of the sun caught inside stopped him. He stood, just looking. He took a deep breath and his shoulders rose in a quiet sigh, a small sinking in his chest barely perceptible. A shadow of cloud floated toward him and the light fell from the circle of sky caught by the pole above. The men tied lines to the pole, changing the sky overhead where the light fell through. Alex stood by the side of the tent unnoticed, yawning as he watched them work. He wanted to rest, to sit for just a minute and rest his legs before going back outside. A wagon was there at the edge of the tent and Alex stepped up into it, just for a minute, he thought, though he knew he should leave.

He'd walked a good three hours this morning before getting a ride, half way to town, the roads empty at that hour of the morning. The farmers were too busy and the fishermen, like his father, didn't care about the circus. Though his mother would have come, Alex thought, if she could. But she never would. There was the baby, and the little ones. The endless bread making. And his father.

In the wagon the boards were worn and rounded under his hands. Feeling the dirt and grit, Alex sat and raised his hands to look at them. Dust of black earth on his palms, not red island clay. He smiled as he touched the dirt with the fingers of one hand. Not from here, this dark earth. Philadelphia, New York. Away. All the places the circus had travelled dusting him. He lay back so the men wouldn't see him and crossed his arms under his head, smelling the sun-warmed boards and the mould of damp dirt.

He shifted his position and the wagon rolled slightly under him. It moved like their boat riding over the sea, the motion that made his brother sick. Alex's stomach tightened as he thought of Reggie there on the boat for the day without him. Having to do Alex's work and his own with his head out over the side, his eyes closed to the water. Back at home Reggie and his father must be headed for shore by now. They would be turning from the view of the open sea. The turn, when the boat twisted back on its wake and moved sideways into the sea, was when Reggie was sickest. Then he would hold as still as possible, not wanting to lean over the edge, be sick as the water splashed up at him. Alex always felt relief then for Reggie, and looked away to watch for the shore for him, but also looked out to the open water, the distance of it expanding into the sky. Trying to see whether he could tell the one from the other, or trying to fool his eye into not knowing. Not seeing the edge of sea or sky, where the one began and the other ended, wanting the world to go on.

He sat up, his shoulders tense. He should have woken Reggie and gotten him to come along. They would have been gone for the day only. He planned to see the show and go back home in the evening. It would've been fun, the two of them on the long walk to town and Reggie seeing things that Alex never noticed, the details of things. He was sure Reggie would've come if he had told him. Why hadn't he?

Because, Alex thought, because Reggie wouldn't have left without telling, without asking. Reggie had been sound asleep when Alex left, Reggie already dreading fishing, dreading their father even more, the oldest son. Everything Alex wasn't.

He'd left before it was light, the house quiet and everyone asleep. He'd gone down the back stairs into the kitchen and gotten dressed. Packed up some bread and put on his shoes in the porch and then left, pushing the screened door shut, the quiet click of it mixing with the sound of the crickets in the night. The road lit by the moon almost full, setting as the sun began to rise. Alex turned west on the road to town; an hour later the sky beginning to blue behind him and the crows cawing.

The men were gone and Alex lay back down, yawned. He pictured himself telling them at dinner, about the horses, the dogs and monkeys, and the acrobats. Skip would laugh he'd tell it so real. And then the kids would play circus for ages afterwards, put on shows for him and Reggie and Fran and their mother. Skip and Mary with the baby dressed up and the dog too. Smiling as he lay there, he saw them standing outside under the lilac tree, the porch their stage. The evening air mild on their faces and the soft red earth of the drive beneath his feet. Smelling the oilcloth in the kitchen off the porch and the boiled fish and potatoes they would have had for dinner. Warm tea towels over sour yeasty bread, a drift of mist crossing the seven o'clock fields. Even now a quiet laugh came from him as he lay in the wagon, his eyes closing, falling asleep, dreaming of home.

Thursday, September 1st. Charlottetown

OUT BEYOND THE HARBOUR IN THE NORTHUMBERLAND Strait the steamship *Victoria* passed early morning fishing boats. George Brown was still asleep, restless, missing his wife. The boat hummed beneath him and the sun slanted through the porthole across his eyes so that he squinted in his sleep. George Etienne Cartier was waking slowly, his stomach grumbling, small French curses coming from his red lips. D'Arcy McGee, used to sea voyages, was already up on deck reading aloud from an orange leather-bound book. And the bottles of champagne filling the hold rolled with the sea, clinking together, eager to proclaim a union, christen them all.

Taking a cold deck shower in the morning sun, John A. Macdonald was the first to see the island sitting red and green in the blue of the sea. In the distance the water made small swells against the island so that the island itself looked as if it were rocking, floating over the waves, moving closer towards them. The cold of the water on his sun-warmed skin made him shiver, raised bumps of flesh, and his skin tingled, tightened with salt. Macdonald hurried as he watched the island. He moved inside to dress, not wanting to miss seeing the approach of the island, rushing. Back out on deck, the harbour appeared more quickly than he'd expected. As if now that they were nearly there, the island found no use in putting them off any longer. The mouth of the harbour suddenly opening in front of them and the land reaching out to them, embracing them, holding them.

ALEX HAD NOT GONE HOME, THE PICTURE of his return, the welcome he'd receive forgotten in the thrill of the circus. He'd helped out like the other boys, all the other town boys, and watched bits of the show in return, home forgotten. Wary to tell them he wasn't from town for fear that they'd send him away, Alex left at night and slept in a church in the square at the south west corner of town, not far from the circus.

On the second night, hidden in a pew at the back of the church, he woke himself as he almost fell off the narrow wooden bench. In his sleep he'd rolled too far, had forgotten where he was, so used to rolling against Reggie in bed. This the only time Alex had slept alone, Reggie always there, always his breath rising and falling on Alex. One never without the other and Alex woke as he nearly fell.

Inside the church it was cool and dark and the early morning sun began to find the panes of stained glass high over the door. From the doorway Alex looked towards the sea A late fishing boat rocked on the wake of a large ship just entering the harbour. He thought of Reggie and his father on their boat at home. He planned to go back today, had been away two days already. Alex left the church, crossed the square, the sun warm on his side, and walked up Pownal Street, away from the water. On Fitz Roy, he walked along the far side of the road, under the pine trees spread on the edge of town. He'd be in trouble, but smelling the trees and the cool morning air of lingering summer reminded him of the smell of home and he shrugged his shoulders, swung his arm out into the air. The things he'd be able to tell them. The things they could do playing pretend. At fifteen, on the cusp of man and child, Alex still dreaming childhood.

He reached the corner. There in the early light sat the circus tent. Something so odd, so impossible that as Alex stopped and looked at it he felt odd himself — a lightness in his chest. He thought it was because he was going home and feeling happy to be going home. He pictured his arrival, walking up the road with Reggie who would have walked down to the corner to meet him. The kids picking late summer blueberries would be hiding in the ditch to surprise him, and the baby sitting on the front step with his mother would wave his hands at him. Alex would walk up the drive, the shells in the soft red earth breaking beneath his feet and he would sit down beside his mother.

Alex's eyes filled, confusing him and he ran across the street wiping his eyes with the back of his hand. Ran in under the lines strung between the circus wagons, the clothes and linens fluttering beneath them, to the banner with the faded blue lettering, "The Snow Brothers Acrobats and Troupe of Acting Dogs and Monkeys," and stopped beside the dogs he'd helped take care of the past two days. The breeze stilling for a moment, the clothes on the line, the banner holding still, the air waiting, turning, blowing in a new wind, a wind from away finding Alex.

AT ELEVEN O'CLOCK, GEORGE COLES AND ALL the delegates in turn, from Prince Edward Island, New Brunswick and Nova Scotia, stood in Province House, in the centre of Charlottetown on this unusually warm September day, with the light pouring in through the windows, and agreed to invite the Canadians to join them. Coles glanced outside. It was cool inside the stone of the building, but knowing the breezy heat rustling the leaves still green, he wanted to be outside. He stifled a yawn. These talks, lazy with lack of interest were ending. They would listen to the Canadians, but right now, longing for the light and the warmth, to get home to this early lunch with a glass of beer in the sun, he didn't think any more of them.

By noon, Coles walked with the others out into the street, crowded even there in the dust red square of Province House, as if everyone who had come for the circus planned to walk every inch of the town, Coles thought. He looked down. Saw the steps of his own feet, a pattern laid in the ground covering and erasing the footsteps there before his. Everything old, the past becoming new again. He the new. Coles looked up, saw the straight noon shadows, the sun in the street and the glare on the leaves of the trees brittle with the end of summer. All of the men hot in the sun and all of them looking forward to this early lunch, the unexpected respite from the talks, a feeling of devil-may-care taking them. Coles himself then, leaving them to go home for lunch, suggested the circus. Why don't they go visit the circus this very afternoon? The Canadians could wait. Really. Everything could wait. And all the men, careless and free, agreed

This break in routine, the early ending of the talks, not what Coles had expected, and this sun everywhere, like summer. Sometimes, sometimes, when that feeling closed in, worry over the business, the counting, endless numbers in his head — he could only think of summer. What he wouldn't give for a lifetime of summer sun and the wind through the clouds that broke the air, broke everything free and him free from his worries. He looked up at the sky, watched a gull overhead. He loved the openness of the outside, when he let himself, loved the wind. Felt now he wanted to jump, to run, like a boy.

And warm yet, though it was the first of September. Thoughts of winter held at bay, a respite from the nagging anxiety that August usually brought. But now, oh now, it seemed like winter could never come. Whistling, he reached home, his hands in his pockets, walking with an easy sway. His own boy Russell running towards him and Coles picked him up, telling him, how about the circus? Shall we go see the circus? Holding the boy's hands so that he could climb his father's legs and somersault through them. Just like a true acrobat, his father said, and the boy laughed, loving his father now, in summer.

WILLIAM POPE WAS THE ONLY ONE WHO hurried away from Province House, headed south towards the harbour to meet the Canadians, give official greeting from the Island government. It was his job, his duty. The others too could have come, but they'd dawdled, as though blinded by the sun, had been made into children by the summer warmth. Pope hurried, thinking of his own child, Joseph, waiting for him at home. Pope had promised to take him to the circus. The first day had passed, and then the second, and now the circus would leave tomorrow and they still hadn't gone. But if he hurried he could be back in time. He smiled at the thought of Joseph — how excited, how impatient he would be. If he'd had time he almost would have thought to bring Joseph here with him, but that would be silly, a boy of eight.

He would have had an adventure though, helped his father row out to the ship in the harbour and then the two of them could have been off and on their way. Now here he was on his own, stepping into the only boat he could find, an old oyster boat with its oars resting in their oarlocks, a barrel of molasses in the stern for ballast, alone, rowing himself out to the *Queen Victoria*.

FROM THE *VICTORIA* JOHN A. MACDONALD WATCHED the shore, looked up at the high white clouds riding the noon hour sun. Lunch was ready below deck but he stayed on deck watching. The harbour and wharf were busy. Families with picnic baskets, mothers in shawls holding the hands of their children, all merrily passed the *Queen Victoria* by. He stood and watched, let his mind drift as he watched the water, the land, all the people arriving. A party happening and they uninvited, the island, the people ignoring them.

Macdonald waited. He needed time. He needed a transformation to take place. He needed a drink. He pulled a flask from his pocket. It was his job, his time. He knew what they expected of him, what he expected of himself, what he knew he could do. He drank, not too much, just enough. It was a fine line: too earnest to be trusted, or too drunk to talk. Macdonald shifted his gaze, followed the line of shore and sky at the harbour's edge. A slivered moon of green along the red of the shore, the sun on his head and shoulders. He sighed as he looked out at the water, the lines along his forehead eased.

As he watched he saw a man, well-dressed, step into a boat and begin to row towards them. The time was now. Neither earnest nor drunk, what could he do? They were to begin here and now, in the sun he wasn't expecting. The water gentle and smelling of summer salt. Here where the island held them and looked away — distracting him, taking him from his task, unprepared and unready. A piece of him as he stood and watched, drifting away, lost to the island.

POPE STOOD ON THE DECK OF THE *Queen Victoria*, fit for royalty, like its name. He looked around him. Aside from the sailor who'd helped him aboard there was only one man on deck. The man turned and Pope and Macdonald both paused for a moment as if neither knew what to do now. Then both men stepped towards each other, but Pope moved sooner, Macdonald a split second behind, off kilter, off-balance. Almost at the same instant, nevertheless, a slight pause making Pope feel unsure.

"William Pope." He paused, extended his hand. "On behalf of the government of Prince Edward Island, welcome to our humble island."

And Macdonald, who had caught himself and stepped forward, extended his hand almost too quickly and nearly hit Pope's arm. "John Alexander Macdonald. We're grateful to have been invited." Macdonald looked out at the curve of the island at the edge of the harbour. On the wharf still more people were arriving. On the deck of the large boat, people were milling about, gathering their parties to go ashore. He could hear laughter and singing. A band he couldn't see played a marching air. On the dock hawkers shouted. Pony rides were being offered and carriages were there to take people up to town or directly to the circus. There was a party everywhere. It made him smile, made him forget his want of a drink. "Such beauty as you have here needs no humility. And besides," nodding out at the ship dislodging more people on the dock, "it looks far from humble."

Pope thought Macdonald's smile was one of amusement: for their small island, for the excitement and the hullabaloo. "It's the circus. First to the island in twenty years. I think the whole island has come to town for it." Embarrassed all of a sudden, the whole of the population here for something so trifling as the circus. And hardly anyone coming for the banquets planned for the Canadians. He turned his head away. Looked around.

"And more besides," Macdonald nodded towards the people on the wharf.

"Yes." Pope looked back at the shore. He wanted to be away. What was he supposed to do? What to tell these men? There was no place for them, the circus goers filled every room, had taken every carriage. No one had thought to hold anything for the Canadians.

"We should go," Macdonald said. Meaning the circus, forgetting why they'd come and wanting an outing like all the others, a simple pleasure.

And Pope, confused as to what Macdonald meant, turned to leave. What was he supposed to make of the men he'd come to greet? The only one who'd seen fit to do it and Joseph at home waiting for him. He turned away from the rail but saw Macdonald still standing, going nowhere.

Macdonald's shoulders raised in a slight shrug. "My son would like it." Forgetting the boy as soon as he spoke, remembering himself as a boy only.

Pope turned back to the rail and looked out at the shore; he thought of the fun he and Joseph would have, pictured the boy's excitement, of how it would create his own anticipation under this September sun. As though they could fall backwards into summer, he and his boy, have a chance to go fishing, go up to the north shore and dig for clams like he'd done when he was a boy. Together with his father, walking the shore finding inlets of sea, the water running out in pretend rivers where they found the tell-tale holes in the sand. He and his father bringing home a black bucket of clams, an impromptu feast for his aunts and uncles come from away. There would be a chance yet. It was not all done, all over, and he smiled as he looked out at the shore. The two men stood together and watched the circus goers, both thinking of idle pleasures, of the summers when they were boys. They felt the warmth of the sun along their shoulders, their hands on the warm wood of the rail. Macdonald with this feeling of ease, wanting food and a drink turned to Pope and smiled as he opened out his arms, "Join us for lunch."

And Pope, feeling as though there were all the time in the world, remembered and forgot Joseph at the same time, and said yes.

From the edge of the tent, the heat of the day at its peak, Alex watched the dogs and monkeys dressed in bonnets and caps, aprons and skirts, and a monkey in pants with suspenders. And he hadn't gone home. One dog in a yellow wig was Goldilocks. Three monkeys played the bears, all carrying about their spoons with their bowls tipped over, spilling if anything had been inside. Another monkey in a small wooden chariot pulled by a dog, was the legend of Ben Hur. Alex laughed as Little Red Riding Hood in a cape gone askew around her neck, dazzled for a moment by the laughter of the crowd, stopped, dropped to all fours and chased the wolf.

And he hadn't gone. Reaching the circus, he'd fed the dogs, watched them play, for all the world like Skip and Mary playing dress-up with their older brothers' and sisters' clothes. Until it all started again, the people arriving, the noise and the excitement. He forgot Reggie. He forgot the new bread and molasses they would have for supper, as though home were no further than the reach of his arm.

He watched the trick horses and the pony with the beautiful girl whose long brown arm he longed to touch. She waved as she rode past him and smiled and nodded to the crowd. But what Alex wanted to see this time, to watch from the very beginning, was the brothers. He made himself look away from the girl and watched for the brothers as they entered the side of the tent, unnoticed by the crowd. The brothers walked so close their shoulders touched, their hands grazed each other, the touch almost invisible. Alex saw Will and Henry separate from Ben and the pair moved to one pole while Ben went alone to the other. The three climbed the ladders next to the poles quickly while the crowd watched the riders. Now when the horses made their final circle of the tent, the crowd would gasp, thrilled by the sudden falling of the brothers as they flew past almost overhead. But Alex wanted something different, not like the crowd. He wanted to know the tricks of timing, the ways of flight. He watched the brothers, saw where they looked, the slight nod of a head and the answer, a hand barely raised. He wanted to see it all, wanted to know when to fall and when to catch.

Alex watched the brothers at the top of their platforms roll their shoulders and flex their arms. Ben reached out to his swing. Across the tent from Ben, Will took the other swing for Henry and held it back, pulled tight for him. Alex saw them look out into the open space, as though feeling the air, testing it like he did the coolness of the water, the pull of the waves. They did not look down and they hadn't looked at each other, gave no indication that anyone else was there high in the tent with them, each quiet, each doing the same thing separately.

And Alex watched. On the ground, where Alex wasn't looking, the ponies did their tricks and the crowd cheered. He had seen that already. Now Alex was alone at the side of the tent, the only one looking up, watching nothing, his breath held. As the horses made their final circle of the tent, he began to count. He saw Henry look at Ben and nod. The two of them pulled back hard on their swings and leapt out. They swung their legs to push themselves forward and up. Alex could see the tension in the muscles of their arms and legs. Could see the glisten of sweat. The noise was the sound of the crowd suddenly hushed, silence the sound of awe and of anticipation as the crowd looked up, watched the brothers as they flew past. The town agog with the acrobatic feats of the brothers on their trapezes, breath the only sound that Alex could hear.

Henry swung above Ben, the two back and forth in opposite time. On the tenth swing, Ben was on his way back in, and Henry was at the farthest reach of his swing in the middle of the tent. Then, Henry let go. He somersaulted out, fell through the air towards the crowd, towards Ben whose swing would intersect with his. And Alex saw that it was wrong. Ben's swing back was too short; Henry was falling through the air to the ground. There were no arms that could reach him. It was all a feat of imagination, a trick of the eye, a trick of belief. The air could hold nothing.

Alex wanted to close his eyes. He heard the crowd gasp, pretend fear and disbelief from those willingly beguiled on a warm and sunny day. They were unknowing, thought it all a part of the show. Alex felt sick. His hands were held tight in fists and his palms cut red in his concentration. He knew that Henry was falling. No net below to catch him, only the flat palm of the ground.

But Will too must have seen it. No, must have felt it before even seeing. He swung out and fell before Alex saw him, adjusting time and space, his line longer. Will fell and grasped Henry's hands which reached out to his brother's as he fell past. Caught at the last moment, in the nick of time.

Alex opened his hands, looked down at his palms, like his hands on the boat cut raw by the fishing lines. Salt water that flailed his skin, his brother sick and his father in the stern, the three of them alone and he the only one who knew how to swim. And Alex wanted the air like water round him. He wanted to fall like the brothers beyond the borders of belief or trust, to fall unstopped through the air and have his hand caught by another. Needing someone who believed with him, a partner in faith, one who would leap with him, save him.

JOSEPH POPE SAT IN A TREE IN the yard, half way up and hidden by the summer leaves, waiting for his father. He'd been waiting two hours already. It didn't matter anymore; the show had started and still he waited. Today, he'd promised, today they would go. Joseph took a twig and held it against the trunk of the tree. Two black ants crawled onto the stick. They walked up it and he pretended they were the acrobats. He turned the stick upside down as the ants, unconcerned, went up and down. He held it so that one ant crawled into his palm, circled it, searching for what? Joseph sighed. He'd barely eaten any lunch he was so excited and now it was nearly tea time.

He shifted, the bark pressed uncomfortably against his legs. He watched the ant on his palm, felt the slight tickling of it as it walked. Joseph looked back at the road. Nothing, no one coming. Holding the twig loosely in his other hand, he watched the single ant crawl along it and then he held it out over the open ground and dropped it. He watched as it hit the ground, the acrobat falling, the crowd below gasping. Joseph gasping too, as if it were real. Pretending to himself, wanting the game. He looked back at his palm and reached his finger out to touch the other ant. So small it tried to crawl onto his finger. It struggled, then caught hold. With his thumb he brushed against it, so small he could barely feel it, could pretend it wasn't there. He brushed harder, and then pressed the ant between his finger and thumb. Opened his hand and looked, only a smudge of black remaining.

September 1st, evening.
Fanningbank, Lieutenant Governor's House

MERCY ANN COLES STOOD ON THE VERANDAH, bright with candles flickering in air. Such a warm wind, only the slightest draft of coolness, a faint warning of fall. The moon falling almost full over the water, the music and noise of the party behind her. A bright night, an unexpected party and she felt light, happy. She leaned her hands against the rail. She wore long gloves that reached up her arms, like her mother's, the ones she'd admired so much when she was small, when she'd longed to be grown up. And now here she was, grown-up. Twenty-six.

She glanced down at herself, at her blue silk dress and she felt beautiful. And young. Even at twenty-six, it was possible, she was still young. She ran her hand down her arm, silk against silk, the material creased in soft folds, left her forearm bare. The air so warm, velvet against her skin and she wished her arms and hands could be uncovered. She thought of Ida on her last visit home. Getting undressed and into bed together as they used to, but something was different about the way she held herself now. That look of being loved, her body possessed, desired.

Mercy looked out at the water. A bit of cool breeze caused a slight shiver, raised goose bumps like after a swim. How nice it would be to swim now, with the moon shading the trees and turning the water into ripples of light. How lovely to float along the surface, to feel the pull of the water on her skin as she pushed against it. Years since she'd swum down at this curve of shore. Where she'd learned to swim, she and her father coming here every afternoon that summer.

They held hands and made up songs and rhymes as they walked. One would start and the other would have to say the next line, rhyming with the first. And then they'd tell stories. And what next? they whispered to each other. Because of that, what next? Inventing lands where the flowers sang. They travelled the world and across to the other shore beyond the strait, and far to the north where the ice was like glass, and the night was all day and the day all night. Describing it as they walked together side by side. Mercy would notice the changes in the path along their way, where flowers had grown, where a river was forged by the rain in the night — a tiny path of water streaming along the pebbles that edged the road. And notice too, the lengthening of the shadows, the changing of the blue of the sky over the water. Summer coming to an end and she hadn't wanted it to. Wanted this to keep going forever.

At the shore together in the shallow water they pushed their hands down on the hard ripples of the sand breaking beneath the sun and kicked their legs out behind them. The water was sun-shallowed and warm against her back. She could feel it now, the softness of this night like the sun and water on her face. And together they walked their hands along the line of shore in the water too shallow to hold her father afloat, not deep enough for him to swim.

As she practiced trying to raise her hands from the ground he would move deeper and swim in a parallel line, getting ahead of her where he stopped and waited. Then sometimes he would stand and stare out at the sea, not shading his eyes as she did to see if she could see the other side, but staring at the openness of it, at the unshaded distance.

On the last day, before the weather turned, August becoming fall, she'd done it. She'd raised her hands and paddled herself along, her legs kicking, moving her forward. She looked to see if he had seen, to tell him, but he wasn't there. She stood and saw him then, out deep in the water. He wasn't swimming but walking forward, the water up to his shoulders and he kept on, walked in deeper. She opened her mouth to call out and couldn't. His back to her, forgotten, as though he were alone. Then he stopped, stood still, as deep as he could go. Mercy's breath held as she saw a wave rise up, splash over his head, and he was gone.

As she stood on the verandah Mercy could hear the music playing and the dancers laughing. She shivered, opened her eyes. The lights in the night seemed very bright. She wanted a soothing darkness, did not want to remember here, now. Too late. Over and done with. Time to move on. Time should move on. She sighed and remembered anyway. She remembered how, as she'd watched, his arms had slowly raised and then slid under the water, the silence of it, the quiet of the sea, drowning a quiet event. Her breath escaped her then, a long release and a silent cry until she'd seen the water push him back and he'd staggered up coughing. Bent over, one hand on his chest and the other wiping his eyes. Then he'd walked past her back up to the shore, sat in the sand and stared out at the sea. She knew he'd forgotten her; she didn't matter; he'd left her. She knew he did not see her as she stood in the water and watched him. And she'd turned and knelt, reached her hands back down to the bottom while the water lapped at her chest and the tears ran down her face, into her mouth and into the water already made salt.

The doors to the verandah opened behind her and the music came louder. She did not want to turn around. The water rippled in the light, looked lovely. She was alone. The same now as then. She closed and opened her eyes. Dry-eyed. A man spoke from behind her. "I believe the next dance is mine, Miss Coles." A Canadian, tones broad and flat, as wide as their land. No sea to stop, or tempt them. The world in front of them. Only thinking now, in a sudden flash, how foolish, trying to drown himself when he knew how to swim. She wanted away and turned quickly. And found John A. Macdonald waiting, his arm out for her to take.

THAT NIGHT ALEX DID NOT LEAVE TO go sleep at the church in the square. He didn't care whether they knew he was a town boy or not, that he had not been home since the circus had come. It didn't matter anymore. What mattered most was the air and the lines through it the brothers travelled.

After the evening performance, once the work was done, Alex went back to the tent alone. He sat looking up at the trapeze seeing the show again. He imagined the brothers as they swung and flew, calculated when one swing would inter-sect another. Saw again Henry's fall and how Will had saved him. Even now Alex gasped as he pictured Henry, the air failing him, dropping him. And he imagined Ben too as he walked along the high wire. The only brother to tight rope walk, the other two on either side, the rope strung between two platforms high over the middle of the tent, and below it, below it, there was nothing.

Alex stood. He walked over to the rope ladder that rose to the high wire. He blinked, rubbed his eyes. Took a breath. The bottom of the rope was at eye level. He grasped it. The rope was looser than he would have imagined; it swung and shifted with his slight touch. When the brothers climbed it, the rope had looked substantial, heavy, as though it were grounded like a real ladder. Alex took hold of the bottom rung in both of his hands, a sure grip, and pulled it tight. He did what he'd seen the brothers do. He pulled and swung himself, turned himself upside down to reach the rung with his feet. He was slight but his arms were strong from hauling fishing lines and he got his legs over the bottom rung. He pulled himself up to standing, the rope ladder swinging slightly. Again he held tightly to the rungs of the ladder and climbed, placed his feet down firmly, to give the ladder weight like the brothers did. But he liked the swing of it, like the boat as it skipped over the waves when the sea was a little rough. Nothing more than that and he smiled, pretended to adjust his cap he wore fishing and hadn't brought.

Alex climbed till he reached the platform and stood. It was high, higher than the tree in the yard, twice as tall as the barn. The highest he had ever been in his life. He walked to the edge of the platform and looked at the rope. He kneeled down and reached his hand out to it. The thick rope was wound tightly as though to hold a ship against the tide pull of the water, as though these small platforms would float away if not held there. He pushed his hand further along on the rope to see what it would be like. He tried to move it and it shifted slightly, moved up and down when he'd expected it to move sideways. Alex stood. He reached his foot out, pushed it against the rope. It didn't move. It was too light a touch, too close to the platform. He stretched a little further, pushed harder as though he would step and the rope shifted up, pushed up against his foot and Alex wobbled. His stomach turned, seasick high in the air. He twisted and grabbed the side of the platform, and the ground moved up and back, a flutter of dance under his half-closed eyes. He saw only the worn circle of grass and dirt far below him. His head was making him sick and Alex closed his eyes, like Reggie, so he couldn't see.

He pictured Reggie leaning out over the side of the boat being sick. Reggie's face white and his eyes closed as they travelled over the water, their father ignoring him. Alex shook his head. He didn't want to picture it. He opened his eyes, looked at the line that stretched across the tent. As wide and open as the sea, and he wanted to be there, in the middle of it. He wanted the openness to surround him with nothing to hold him in, contain him.

He stood up straight on the platform, stepped forward to the edge and looked out, then knelt down and grasped the rope. He moved forward till his knees were at the very edge of the platform. Glancing at the far side, he took a breath, did not look down. Adjusting his grip he let his legs fall over the side. A gasp escaped him, his own weight at that height pulled him hard, tugged him towards the ground. He tightened his grip. The rope was thick and it was difficult to hang on to. He realized he was holding his breath as though he were below water and he opened his mouth, breathed deeply and it calmed him. On one side of him the platform was in reach.

He only had to extend his arm and grasp it. And to the other side, nothing.

Raising his head he looked up at the line. He inched his hands forward till he was free of the platform and hung there with nothing on either side. The ceiling of the tent flapped in the night breeze and the wind drifted through the circle of sky above his head. He could see a piece of cloud turned white by the moon, the air blowing cool over him like a current of water. A sea of air surrounding him, and Alex wanted to walk it, walk through the air, as effortless as floating. He pulled himself up, fear and excitement making him shake, until he sat on the wire, in the middle of the air, about to stand.

Alex took a deep breath, held it a minute and slowly exhaled. The rope was firm under him, the edge of the boat as it tilted away, as big as that, as wide and firm as that. Alex had walked along the side of the boat many times. A dance, a shuffle of his feet, keeping his balance as the water moved fast below him and the boat in a bob up and down. This air far more still than water. Always best not to look down, whether air or water, and Alex did not look down. He took another slow breath in and out. The distance back to the platform no more than the width of their boat. He stood.

Mercy danced with Macdonald, small talk of the island, of the circus, only half the dance before he stopped, let go of her hands and bowed. Her father stood there waiting.

"You look beautiful, grown up, and I hadn't noticed. I wanted to dance with you." Her father smiled at her. The night was so warm, he thought how lovely it would be to go for a walk down to the shore. Like the beginning of summer, and all the possibilities the beginning of summer brought. "You don't mind do you?"

Seeing him smile at her, so happy, she smiled back and kissed his cheek. Everything else was so long ago.

"There are more people here than I imagined," he said. They danced looking out at the room. "We have so much, nothing better than here." He loved the excitement in the air, the circus and the Canadians together seeming like one big event. "The weather even, see what weather we offer them," puffing out his chest. As though nowhere else in the Maritimes was having the same wonderful and prolonged summer.

"Yes." She paused, "Warm enough to swim even."

"What a night for it! Get a party together, drive to the North shore." It would be wonderful, he thought. If not tonight, then tomorrow. He would arrange it. Counting the number of carriages they would need, planning it out in his head.

"There is the shore right here, too." She looked at him, "Remember?"

Continuing his planning, calculating the numbers as they danced. "That's a long time ago now." He didn't want to remember.

She felt him pull away from her. It made her feel not loss but the fear of loss. That tug of anxiety every time he left: Mercy always longing for more than he could give.

"Remember when we would go to the north shore . . . ?" she wanted him to remember with her, to stay dancing with her, the reckless love of a child, still wanting, hoping. The sun and the warmth, the glorious days when they would all go together, take picnics, he and her mother relaxed and happy. Canvas awnings up against the wind and she and Ida hot in the shelter of the dunes. "You would go in swimming and we would go too. Run after you into the water." She smiled at him,

"And mother would only let us go up to our waists and you would swim out deep. Swim straight out into the deep water where mother would never let us go." Mercy remembered how she would pretend close to shore that the water was over her head and the ground far below, the water endless around her. "And I always wanted to go with you." She was speaking quickly, felt breathless and stopped. "Why couldn't I go with you? I wanted to so much." She stopped dancing as she asked. She wanted now an answer from him. She had been left. He had tried to drown himself while she was just a child left alone at the shore. What was she supposed to do? Always leaving and never taking her, where she wanted to go, with him.

"Don't ask silly questions, Mercy." He looked away, saw his wife who smiled at him and waved. He waved back.

Mercy felt as though the ground sucked at her feet. Her father continued to dance and she missed step, so that for a moment it looked as though he would move on, keep dancing without a partner, move across the dance floor by himself. The music ended and he left her then saying, "You can only do your best. I always did my best." Mercy stood as though lost, an unknown grief. A loss that wasn't. Left alone again, set adrift in the middle of the floor by herself.

Friday, September 2nd. Morell

AT FIVE-THIRTY IN THE LATE AFTERNOON, REGGIE could see the sun through the kitchen's back window. In an hour it would be red. A sailor's delight. The next day would be good for fishing, but Reggie wasn't thinking about fishing. The day had been warm again and it was hot in the kitchen where they were eating dinner. Warmest by his mother and Fran, closest to the stove. Fran at the end of the table with the baby in his chair next to her, the sun touching the top of her hair, a breeze blowing in warm through the window. The small kids were pulled up close against the wall at the back of the table, his father at the head to his right. A slow gap that no one spoke of on Reggie's left where Alex had always sat between him and their mother.

The first three days they'd searched the shore and dragged the lake. Reggie watched himself as though he were someone else, not *his* brother gone, lost, not *him* searching. There was a fog in his head that wouldn't leave. As childish as Skip, he thought, believing Alex would come home, just step inside the door, as though he hadn't disappeared, gone just pretend. He shook his head, picked up his fork, turned a piece of potato. "There's to be a parade in town tomorrow," he said. Fran and the kids looked at him. His father kept eating. Reggie looked at Fran, at his father, then continued, "The Tenant Leaguers. Going from across the island."

"Have they not got more important things to hand at this time of year?" his father said. "They're in want of a real taste of work." He went on eating his dinner and didn't look up. He and Reggie were both tired, working hard these past four days. Neither knew what they would do now that Alex was gone.

Reggie held his fork, looked at it, at the fish and potatoes on his plate. "There's nothing much more important than owning your own land. We've got to own the land if things are ever to change here." He looked at his father. "It's our island isn't it?"

His father looked at him then looked around the table. "They gather the crops, don't they? Same as us and the sea." He looked back down. "You don't see us badgering to own the sea do you? Some good that would do us anyway. As if you could own the sea." He laughed, brushed his hands and reached for the plate of bread.

Reggie looked out the window across from him. "It's not the same." He thought of the water as it shifted and moved. That it couldn't be trusted to hold still, how it made him sick. "You can't keep water, but you can own the land you work." Getting red, angry. "What sense does it make for us islanders to go on working this land and then paying to work it, too?" He turned to look at his father. "Don't you care?" He heard his own voice loud, blunt. The rest of them were silent.

His father looked up. His face was clean shaven, creased — water worn. Blue eyes too, like Reggie's. The only two with blue eyes. He took his knife, looked down to butter his bread. "Well what do you care Reg? You're not a farmer. You're a fisherman. Like me. Like my father and his father." He looked at Reggie again, his face dismissive, calm. "The Lord's own profession you know Reg. Remember that."

Reggie looked down at his hands. Washed raw and clean. A fine red cut across his palm from the fishing line. He shook his head. "No," surprised himself by the words coming out. "No, I'm not a fisherman."

His bread and knife still in his hands, his father looked at Reggie. "Well what would you be then Reg, if you're not a fisherman? Seeing as how you fish." A slow drawl.

Reggie raised his hands from his lap and put them on the table. He looked at his father. "I'll not fish again." He pushed his chair back, stood. "I'll not go out on the boat anymore." Not knowing what to do now. He'd planned to tell them he'd be away for the day with his uncles, his mother's brothers, farmers all, joining the march. Gone for the day only. He stood there, his cheeks hot, his face flushed. What was he doing? But he couldn't take it back now. He'd meant it. He wouldn't fish again, wouldn't go out on the water that turned his stomach inside out, sick over the side of the boat again and again. It was finished.

Reggie stared at his father who did not look up. "I'm going to the parade tomorrow. To tell them this island is ours. It's more than can be said for you, father. We can have more." He heard his voice break. "I want more," looking around the room, at the fish he hated cold on his plate, "than this."

"You'll not go," his father said, as he slowly put his knife down. He looked at his bread, took a bite, ignored Reggie.

"Yes father, I will." Reggie turned away from the table. Moved around his chair, his back towards Fran who stood, her hand reaching across the table towards him.

"Reggie," his father said, making him jump, hesitate.

Reggie turned then towards the porch door, the baby started to cry and his mother turned towards it, away from him.

"You'll not be wanted here if you leave, Reggie. Leave and don't bother coming back."

Reggie stopped. He shook his head and strode across the porch, the click of the door behind him, soft, slow. And his father's words on top, "Frances. Get me some tea." Reggie heard her turn back from the door, stopped by his father's voice. Walking fast, he crossed the field down to the main road, his hands tightening into fists.

In the house his father stood and walked into the front room. He took down the chain of wooden links he was carving. He was famous for carving unbroken links from a single piece of wood. He took his whittling knife from his pocket, sat in his chair and held the wood in his hand, gauging where next to cut. It was the sea, not the land, that took everything it wanted. Hope drowned, turned mute. He wiped his forehead, studied the wood. Saw how the grain wove in and out through the links. He cut a smooth slice, carved steadily, did not look up. Reggie would be back. The links joined one within the other, by their nature, he thought. It was within the wood itself, in the nature of the wood. He just had to find it. He stopped, looked again at the wood and then closed his eyes. In his nature too, he couldn't escape it. The sea. The chain lying over his lap and over the edge of the rocking chair he'd made himself, rose and fell with the slow rock of his chair. He held the wood in his hand while the rocker stopped, the link between his fingers, snapping.

Friday, September 2nd, evening. North Shore

MACDONALD CLIMBED, SMELLING THE SWEET GRASS, THE marram that covered the dunes while the sand, turned cool, rolled out from beneath his bare feet, his back to the wind blowing his hair into his eyes. He stopped to rest and looked up at the sky.

The moon stood full over the water, its light falling across the island. It fell first here along the north shore where the wind was blowing. Windier and wilder than the Charlottetown shore, round and open with sand and bays, inland lakes reached through cranberry bogs and salt marshes where the sea ran in and trapped itself. Oysters in the salt tide rivers pulled out by the tide.

Not yet late, the short path of the light found the men who walked west along the edge of the shore. Coles led the way, this night time excursion under the September summer moon.

High in the sky the moon lit the curve of the tallest dune and showed the lone man climbing its spreading slope.

Macdonald breathed hard as he climbed. He leaned forward, using his hands to steady himself and help him climb. He turned as he reached the top and faced into the wind looking out over the moonlit water. The water appeared to rise as it rounded the earth, reached up to the sky. The ocean and wind seemed to John A as if they began right here where he stood bending into the wind.

Everything was happening, without effort, without will even. The future was here, right here in the waves breaking on the shore, pulled by the tide. The future becoming now, as unstoppable as the sea and he not having to do anything at all. Everyone and everything caught in the tide of the future.

Macdonald raised his hand, waved at those below on the shore, felt sure of himself again. The island was bringing him everything he needed. No need for drink, for distraction, no loss. He was everything and everything was now. Everything falling together, his for the taking. And he would. He knew what he wanted. The wind and the water and the island meeting him here, joining him, whole again. He called to the men below, the wind and the water drowning out his voice as he cried out in exaltation.

TWELVE MILES TO THE EAST OF THE road that carried Macdonald and the rest of the delegates back to Charlottetown, the moon's light fell in through the open door of a barn on Reggie curled up in the hay of an empty stall. His hands unclenched as he fell into sleep dreaming of him and Alex together at the parade, Alex and Reggie never apart, the two of them side by side, Alex safe and undrowned by Reggie's side. They would go together; together they were strong. Reggie imagined their mother and Skip and Fran waving to them as he and Alex walked past, all of them happy. And Reggie fell asleep, the moonlight and sweet smell of summer straw covering him.

TRAVELLING FURTHER YET, MOVING ACROSS THE ISLAND, the moon found the circle of bent grass where the circus tent had been and a spill of dust as the last of the wagons headed down Queen Street to the docks. The moon, beginning to set, left a trail of light over the water that ended at Alex waiting by the Princess of Wales for the circus to arrive.

He watched the line of moon over the water, wanting to walk it. He'd practiced these past two days along imaginary lines, stepping with precision, each step a line of air to be calculated. Determining the projection of his foot, finding the right spot to land, his arms and head placed just so. Alex closed his eyes. He could feel the moonlight on his face, the wind easy, like when they went fishing so early it was still night. He opened his eyes and stepped to the edge of the pier, the water slipping in dark swells on his left and under the wood-tarred boards of the dock, the slip slap sound of rain beneath his feet. Turning back towards the moon, he stretched out his arms and began to walk along the edge of the pier. He closed his eyes again, felt the light on his face, the air on every part of his body, noticed his own breathing. Knowing even breath itself was a weight that could hold him down, upset his balance. Alex walked slowly forward with his eyes closed along the edge of the pier, the soft shush of the water under him like the sound of the crowd far below the brothers.

He imagined walking out over the water in the night. Wondered, if he didn't open his eyes, if he didn't know, could he step out past the end of the pier, walk this line of moonlight? The wind blew against his face, warm — unbelievably warm. So warm he could forget it was nearly fall, that school would start soon. That winter would come and the roads be so thick with snow that they would have to stay home, storm-stayed in their kitchen refuge. Playing cards, laughing and joking, the warm smell of tea and bread, their father playing his fiddle. But here, now, as he walked alone in the mild air, so open and free and the night to himself, it was as if this could never end. Nights upon nights he would walk lines through the air like the brothers. He would cross the country with them along rivers and lakes that pushed out here to this strait, to his island. Walking still forward, keeping his balance on the wide edge of the pier, Alex wanted to walk out and out and out. And away.

Saturday, September 3rd. Charlottetown Harbour

IN THE MORNING THE FARMERS FROM ACROSS the island met at the foot of Great George in Charlottetown. Five hundred men and boys strayed down Water Street and over the wharf and docks. Reggie was with his uncles and cousins on the pier, busy with people crowding them close. He turned to look behind him, careful of where he stood. Seeing the water and unable to look away, he watched a ship headed for the harbour mouth.

"What are you fellows up to, then?" a boy asked. "You're too late for the circus. It's come and gone." He and another boy pointed to the ship leaving the harbour. The boys watched the ship and Reggie looked too. He didn't care about the circus, hadn't given it a passing thought. He watched it, sorry it was leaving, though he didn't know why. Still, he watched with them, his back to the farmers as they gathered and moved into their places in line. Just before the ship was gone from sight, Reggie turned away and answered the boy. Turned away from the water, from the boat leaving, and pointed to the men gathering.

"They are . . . We are," he included himself in the motion of his hand, "the Tenants' League. We are all of us come to tell the government they won't pay their rents anymore." Reggie took the tin horn his uncle had given him, raised it in the air and gave it a shake, blew into it, a small sound barely heard in the noise of the crowd. The line of men and boys began to move forward then as the breeze picked up and one by one all the farmers lifted their horns and blew into the air. The horns tinny and open, the sound taken by the wind, travelled over the water, to the *Queen Victoria*, waking John A. Macdonald from his champagne sleep, and to the circus boat leaving. A fanfare of tin horns blowing it away.

Reggie moved forward with the parade of men, the music of the horns, the chanting and singing of the men filled his ears, his head, his body. One hundred from his end of the island alone, from St. Peter's Bay, Morell and Morell Rear. A street of tilled lines stretched out in front of him, the breeze blowing them forward, up from the harbour. As if rising from the sea a field of men moved in this slow waltz up the street, their voices caught on the wind and blown before them, the song and the wind moving up the street. The morning sun shone warm on them, gleamed off Reggie's horn into his eyes and made him look down. The red of the earth turned pink on his dark boots. Like the zinnias in his mother's garden at home, he thought, like a party.

They marched up past King Street away from the water, towards Dorchester. Contained within the street, the horns took on a more solid ring, echoed off the buildings and played in Reggie's head like his father's fiddle as they danced. He moved to the rhythm of it, all of them together flowing forward pushed by the wind music. Another block up and Reggie could glimpse Province House at the top of the road. Empty yet, though the farmers didn't know it. The delegates were only now rising from their moonstruck sleep while the field of men in a dance of wind moved up the road.

Reggie looked to his left. Crowds of people thronged the street. They called out to the farmers, sang with them, cheered them on. He raised his horn, blew loudly, raised his hand and waved. Five hundred people sang together. He stopped to listen for a moment, closed his eyes, wanted to hear the sound surround him. Feel the noise against his skin, in his very bones, everyone here calling for land, everyone the same. The sound of them erasing his father's voice. His eyes still closed he stepped forward, bumped into the man in front of him. He'd stepped too close with his eyes shut and he opened them quickly now and stepped back. Looked again to his left and right to place himself. They had just passed the Catholic church when Reggie turned back with a sudden motion. The steps of the church were filled with watchers, and there, on the lowest step, he was sure of it, stood Alex. Here at the parade.

Reggie thinking he sees Alex everywhere, out of the side of his eye. Impossible to believe that a brother always there, isn't.

Reggie raised his horn, called out. Turned to his cousin to see if he saw Alex too, but his cousin looked forward, marched on. Reggie moved his head, tried to keep Alex in his sight. He stepped sideways to get out of the line, and couldn't, crowded with so many of them. He pushed his way around the men and the pitchforks, ducked under someone's arm. He looked again. Alex had moved, was walking with the farmers as they marched up the street. Reggie called again, knew he couldn't be heard. He stumbled over someone's foot, and when he reached the side of the street he walked fast trying to catch up with Alex. Reggie's arms were swinging and he smiled at the thought of Alex. He reached him just as Alex turned away. It wasn't Alex at all. The boy didn't look anything like Alex, just his dark hair and the way he stood. He walked away not even noticing Reggie. Reggie's arms fell to his side. He was left standing alone and Alex still gone. Reggie's ghost brain, a constant reminder, a constant forgetting. His eyes blurred while the parade of farmers moved past up the street without him, his place lost.

LULLED, STILL DREAMING, THE MOTION OF A boat over water so familiar beneath him, Alex didn't wake as the steamer carrying the circus back across the strait to Shediac was set free from her moorings. The sun warmed him, falling across his face and shoulders as he rolled over, his back against the cage of the brothers' dogs. The sound of them as one began to bark, woke him and he sat up surprised to find himself out in the harbour. Hidden by their cages, he'd gone to sleep the night before intending to wake early and leave the ship before it sailed. He should go home. He hadn't gone — he'd waited for the circus to arrive at the wharf; he'd meant to say goodbye — but he'd stolen aboard, hidden himself by the dogs, believing he would rise and leave early in the morning. But he hadn't. He didn't get up now either, even though the boat was leaving and him with it. He sat there, the water so still the big boat seemed motionless under him. So still he thought they must be stopped, must not be moving at all though he saw the shore moving away from him.

Finally Alex stood and walked to the rail. He watched the water make eddies against the ship. The two moved against each other, water and ship, as though they were both leaving. He heard a strange sound. It was field horns, he realized, used to call the men in for dinner. The sound transposed seemed as though it came from the water itself. It called now as though urging the island to come, to follow their ship, not to stray too far. Come now, the water called to the island. But Alex saw the island drifting away.

The breeze picked up, blew against him as they moved into the open. He'd never seen the island from this side before. The green of the land rolling into short banks of red clay and the water lying at its feet as though there were no tide to toss or pull it, to draw them back in or pull them away. Not like his shore, where the water ruled the land and the dunes and sand gave way to the waves, the tide of the whole Atlantic pulling against the shore.

And not like on their fishing boat where he would watch for home, the piece of shore where he swam. The line up from it: red dirt road and brown-eyed susans, berries in the ditch and a line of fir trees that stood to the west of the house. Not that he could see any of that from their boat. Just that he could locate it in his mind. See where the land travelled up from the sea to their house, knew the walk to the shore, almost half of it through the grass and dunes before coming to the sea or home, depending on which way he was going. Nothing like that here. So different from what he knew that he didn't think of home.

He turned away to face into the wind, the salt of the air on his tongue. Loving it, he couldn't help himself, when they moved out into the open, the wide expanse of sea and sky inviting them onward, the horns behind him muted now, then silent, forgetting him.

Every which way he looked Alex could see only the open water and clouds of eastern light moving like waves across the sky. He turned back for a moment, the island so soft and low that the horizon covered and hid it now. No arm of land showing, no finger or hand outstretched to him, the island gone from sight, from view, gone from belief. Nothing to pull him back and Alex turned again, leaned forward into the wind, watching the open sea.

REGGIE FELL ASLEEP ON THE RIDE HOME from town. It was late in the evening by the time the farmers left the parade and headed east back up the island. He turned away from his uncle, shaking his arm. "Wake up son, you're home. Come on boy." Reggie sat up, and still half-asleep and rubbing his eyes, remembered. Up the shore road, he could see the house. A light in the kitchen waited and he felt a happiness, slow like a dream — there was home and he was safe. And slowly he understood — that it was the light for Alex, who still wasn't home, still unfound. A light for Alex and to let all know they were waiting for him, searching. Not for him, not for Reggie, who'd left home willingly, who'd crossed his father. Not a sign for him, no one waited, no one wanted him.

"Tomorrow," Reggie said and looked away from the house, away from his uncle. Reggie rubbed his eyes, continued, "It's too late now. They'll be by after church, they said. I forgot to tell you. Yeah, I forgot." He lay awake, watched up at the sky as the stars came out and the moon set. He thought of the boy at the parade, not Alex. Not Alex who had disappeared in the night while Reggie slept. Reggie hadn't even woken, hadn't felt the shift in the bed, the weight of Alex leaving. Alex's breath on his skin as they lay so close together in the night, gone. As though there and not there were the same. And Reggie turned away from the others, looked out at the fields that lined the road. Only a mile wide these fields, some of them just a fringe of land that hid the ocean, but he knew it was there, the tide going out now, a habit of sea he couldn't forget. Reggie felt its pull as though he were in the water and he drew his arms close to himself. Thinking of Alex and not wanting to, his brother gone, and he, Reggie had gone, too. Gone and unwanted. Gone and searched for, waited for. Both gone.

Sunday, September 4th. West End House, Charlottetown

LIPS RED WITH RASPBERRY, MERCY TRIED NOT to smile. She watched the men play chess, the boards laid out on tables set around the long length of lawn that stretched almost down to the water. She shaded her eyes to watch the move Mr. Brown made, hoping to hide her face from Colonel Gray who, in an attempt to be chivalrous, was explaining the rules to her.

She already knew how to play. Not common for a girl to play, but her father had taught her that, too. She looked at him where he stood with Dr. Tupper from Nova Scotia. She could hear her father laugh, his arms spread wide and expansive. He was too loud. She wanted him to hold his arms down, be calm. Overexcited and glorying in it — the weather now, summer extending into September, the praises being showered on his island. Every morning he talked of what the Canadians had said, of what they had to offer. This morning he'd berated the farmers for their parade. If only they understood the possibility, the potential the Canadians were bringing. A union of the Canadas, the money to buy out the landlords. They could own their own land. The landlords were the blight that held the island back, she could hear him say again as his voice rose louder yet. She looked away, could still hear him. What more could they want? almost shouting. They would see though, understand, the land would be theirs. She sighed. Calm, barely a breath of wind. It was hot and she raised her hand to push her hair off the back of her neck.

Her father stopped and she looked towards him and Tupper. She saw him look out to the water and pause, watching it.

The water a constant reminder, George Coles thought, that they were islanders, that the sea held them. Swimming was his attempt to have some control, make peace with it, so that it could never demand, or take too much. Though there had been times. He pushed the thoughts to the back of his mind. He turned away. Now there were the talks, the idea of a grander, bigger country, and a grander, bigger island. He looked back at Tupper with a shrug of his shoulders. An apology, for his excitement, for his volubility.

Mercy watched him, saw how he seemed to shrink when he turned back to Tupper, how he'd stopped talking, his small shrug. She wished he would walk with her down to the water and they could pretend like they used to that they could see the far shore. Or imagine the island was a ship that could sail the ocean, take them anywhere they wanted. Everywhere the island, everywhere home. Knowing now how foolish it was, how foolish he was, that he couldn't be trusted. Her father. That was the rub. Her father, who had taught her to swim, who was too loud, who'd left her at the shore. And yet, there it was — she loved him.

She excused herself from the Colonel and walked across the lawn to them. Coles looked up and smiled, opened his arms. Dr. Tupper bent his head toward her. He had the air of a man who thinks he could make love with you. She'd seen him taking the women's hands, and taking hers now, a slight obsequiousness, bowing his head so that his eyes remained raised, rested on the line on her dress. The kind of man who thought women would always welcome him.

Mercy turned to her father. "Even the berries are good," she said and looked down to the water. She smiled at him, "You are right. We are in the midst of summer yet." A beautiful afternoon, only two o'clock, the shadows making shade from the sun, not lengthening into evening yet. She wanted to take his hand.

Tupper turned to her. "What do you think of the union proposal, Miss Coles? The women, of course, no matter what we men say, will decide on the proposal in the end." He looked away from her, waved his arm carelessly at the people gathered on the lawn.

"I know my father thinks highly of it. Of course we are an island," she looked away, "and there is no physical process, or will, that can unite us as one." True, she thought, they could never be one, never be the same. Different and separate, always not knowing what the others knew. Islanders knowing the whole of small.

The two men laughed. "Yes, yes, you're right, Mercy," her father said. "Nevertheless, . . . " and he turned back to Tupper and Leonard Tilley who joined them.

Mercy left and walked down to the edge of the grass. The lawn ended in a small inlet, a tiny bay in front of the house where she stood and looked out over the water. Sometimes on a clear day, it seemed as if they could see the mainland, the New Brunswick shore. Could believe that the world extended beyond the borders of the island. Here, as she looked, there was only water and waves, a gull close to shore, everything the same. She leaned down wanting to feel how cool the water was and reached out her hand. Stood again, one wet gloved hand raised in surprise.

Standing on the grass below the porch of the house, Macdonald looked at the people on the lawn and smiled. The sun warm on his hand holding his plate of cake and the summer smell of cut grass in the air. He lifted a raspberry with his fork and ate it. Even a tinge of tart, not over ripe yet, still in the bloom of youth. Like the Canadas, he thought, the potential, the beauty of youth. What a country this could be. And the eastern colonies were joining, the swell of momentum taking them all. Fruit falling ripe, easy. He looked down at his cake and took another bite, held a berry in his mouth sweet against his tongue.

They were in the process of creating the future, the future past. Yes, he'd make sure to say that in the speeches tomorrow. The two created at the same time, future and past. They were, he was, creating history, everything starting new, now, with him. Here on this island separated from the mainland, the possibilities opened wide, like the spread of the sea in front of them, in front of him.

He thought of his speech to the Easterners today, his saga of the greatness of the land. To appeal to them, to show them what could be. The Canadas needed them. He needed them. He raised his fork, ate more cake. Her fertility knew no bounds. Three and a half million children, and 175,000 more born every year. The Maritimers liked it, they liked him. Six hundred and twenty-eight vessels birthed from her loins in the past year alone. Ships that sailed forth, carrying with them their mother's limitless produce. Grain grown white against the blue of her eyes, fish from her lakes and the salt of the St. Lawrence worth ten million dollars a year. Her tresses, trimmed from the forests of Canada East, New Brunswick and Nova Scotia sold for fifteen million dollars. Together, imagine it, greater than any country in Europe. Together, he could do that. He saw it, pictured the glory of it.

Macdonald breathed in deeply. A drink would be nice, a toast. It was fitting, there ought to be a toast. He looked around the lawn for McGee, but didn't see him. What a time, what a place. It made him think of his home in Kingston overlooking the lake. Remembering the house made him think of his naps on the porch, the sound of insects in the heat of the sun. Warm and relaxed, a drink and a nap is what he wanted. He raised his hand and shaded his eyes. It seemed a long time since he'd been home. He missed it, this island time, almost like home, almost.

Something beyond him, beyond them, was happening. He looked down to the shore, watched the waves as they rolled into and over each other. Like yesterday on the *Victoria*, everyone's glasses filled with champagne, toasting each other — the Maritimers and the Canadians from East and West together, as the waves rose and fell under them. Champagne spilling out from the top of his glass over the edge of the ship and into the sea, proclaiming union. The sea christened with champagne. Years stalled and stalemated till now, the country, the time coming together as if of its own accord. All of them pulled along since this past June in Quebec, regardless of Brown, or himself. With or without him. Unnecessary, unresponsible, free. He closed his eyes, sighed. He turned towards the house, the sun shining into the windows yet and Macdonald went up onto the porch and went inside.

Mercy, seeing nothing and wanting to see more, walked back towards the house. A higher vantage point, she thought, the widow's walk might provide a broader view. She wondered whether even Summerside would be visible from the top of the house. The land from here curved up and away from town, swept inland. The island pulling back from the New Brunswick shore, wanting to escape the gaze of the mainland, Mercy thought, not wanting to be caught, wary to be held.

She climbed the stairs to the top of the house; the sun from the windows of the room above her filled the space on the stairs. Sunlight and heat magnified by the glass. Wanting the feel of the sun on her arm, Mercy took off her gloves then leaned against the wall. The warmth and smell of the heat made her close her eyes, and loving the feeling of light on her face, she climbed the last two stairs with her eyes still closed.

She stepped into the room and jumped, startled by a voice, not expecting anyone to be there.

"Good afternoon, Miss Coles." John A. Macdonald was facing the door, holding his hat and unable to offer his hand. His left hand lowered from his jacket, returning the flask as he'd heard her on the stairs. He'd seen her pause and take off her gloves and he'd stepped back further into the small room, looking behind him as though someone might be there to surprise him too.

They were too close to curtsy or bow and there was no room for her to step back without going down the stairs. He smiled, looked away. He was so close it was as though he were waiting for her, she thought, with his hat held in his hand. His hair falling over his forehead, too thick, like a boy's, unruly. Such an ugly man.

Macdonald, held by the warm stillness of the afternoon sun and the niceness of the drink, thought he should go and stayed. Unable to step past Mercy without stepping into her. He moved his hat to his other hand, shrugged.

Standing like that with his arms lowered made her think of their dance. His negligent air and small talk, his hand so inconsequential on her back. She felt the warmth of it, as if they were dancing now, standing so close, the room so small. The dust falling in the sun between them, and her gloves in her hand.

"Hello, Mr. Macdonald. I didn't expect to find anyone here." She turned to look out the window. She could see nothing more than the line of shore below her, a drift of cloud along the horizon pretending to be land. She looked back at him, "And there is no one with you, no one hiding behind you?" She moved her head as though to look. "A shepherd who has left his flock." She turned back to the window.

Macdonald laughed. "You as well, are here by yourself. Or were expecting to be."

Mercy looked at him and then back at the water. "I wanted to see the mainland. Somehow a land so big ought to be visible and I wanted to see if I could see it from here." She raised her hand to shade the glass, saw bubbles like water caught in the window, the texture of glass, not water against her bare skin.

Macdonald too, turned and looked. He could feel the heat from her bare arm, her sun warmed skin. "Can you?" As though he himself were not looking at the same view and that she being from here could see something that he couldn't. The process of vision different for the two of them.

Mercy smiled. "No. Nothing but sea. It's as though Prince Edward Island is all there is." She sighed, barely audible. Nothing more to see or believe. She lowered her hand, looked without trying to see. The world beginning and ending here, the island everything.

"Yes, lucky you." The peace of it, how for the past week time had seemed to rest. He stared out at the water. It would be nice to swim, he thought. How long had it been since he had? He saw Mercy shift and thought she had turned away from the window, was impatient and wanted to leave. He turned towards her.

Mercy looked at him; he didn't understand. Why would he? A mainlander, from a land without end that spread forward and back, with nothing to stop it. Ignorant of islands. "Have you been down to the shore yet, Mr. Macdonald? Have you been in the sea? Or are you and your company too busy for such slight entertainment?"

He saw her watch him. It was so warm and still. "Ah, Miss Coles, I would love to see all the shores of your isle." He raised his arm and moved his hand across the window. "It is beautiful, more beautiful than any other I have seen. Red soil and blue sea, a brilliant and unlikely combination." He stopped and looked at her. "But no, I have not swum." His face stilled for a moment. "Though I often dream of it sleeping on the *Victoria*." Remembering his dream of the night before, of he and Isa in the blue of the Caribbean sea. He swimming and showing her in the warm and shallow water how to float. That was the last time, seven years ago. Just before she'd died.

Mercy glanced at him and out the window. "Well then, you haven't really seen the island at all, if you haven't swum from her shore." She shrugged her shoulders not looking at him. Ran her finger over the glass. "You need to feel an island's borders, the lines of its shape, if you are to know and under-stand an island." She turned to look at him, a mock serious frown on her face.

He looked at her and laughed again. "You are right, Miss Coles." He nodded. "I will do that. I'll make sure that I swim before I leave here." She was leaning slightly back to look up at him and his eyes met hers in this silly banter. She saw the reflection of herself, an island in the sea beyond held in his eye. And he looked too, could have glanced and looked away without noticing, but didn't. A coincidence of vision and time. They looked into each other's eyes and did not look away. Both caught in the other's gaze, each caught for a moment in the other.

The moment lengthened till hearing someone climbing the stairs they both shifted, noticed how they were leaning almost imperceptibly one towards the other, each knowing the other saw, both shifting back.

Sunday morning Reggie went with his uncles and cousins to the church in Morell Rear. The small building was warm white in the sun, set in the midst of farmland, the crows raucous on fence posts, and Reggie breathed in deeply as he got down from the wagon. He'd always liked it when they came out here to his mother's family, a summer feast held on the farm and all of them spending the day together. His cousins would pull him out to the back field. Smoking makeshift cigarettes, getting dizzy and lying down on the ground at the edge of a field. Heads of summer barley greening in the sun, dragonflies over the ditch at the side of the road and butterflies on blue larkspur. The smell of it like another land to Reggie, not salt, not water, not sea. Just grass and crops, sweet clover and the tang of cow dung, the world a wonder of blue sky and land.

Reggie smiled as he looked at the fields before he went into the church. Darker inside than out but still sunny, no dark glass to shade the light. He sat in the pew beside his aunt. She looked at him and touched his arm. His mother's sister who'd married a farmer, like her brothers, like her father. His mother the only one who'd gone astray, marrying a fishing man, moving away from the land, towards water. And where had it gotten them, Reggie wondered? Sitting in the church, sun-drenched flies a drowsy buzz sermonizing in summer, giving gentle warnings like the priest who didn't mention the parade, only talked homilies, don't go too far, don't ask for too much, let God's will be done. Be content, be still, be here, lulling his flock.

Reggie's neck was tight with tension. Too far, he had gone too far. Left his father, left his brother. But what else could he do? And what of his father? Alex gone and Reggie had let him leave, and now no sons to fish. If there are no sons, there is no father. He should go home, apologize, let God's will be done.

His shoulders rose. God's will. What was God's will that he should listen to a father who didn't care? He ran his hand over his forehead. He was made for something different. Impossible to account for God's will. Alex disappeared and what was he, Reggie, to do? He and his father had done the only things they could, neither one able to do anything differently. It was over and done. He didn't belong. There was no place for him.

He heard again his uncle's words at breakfast. "Two sons in the space of a week, Reggie. It isn't right." Reggie held himself stiffly, looked away from his uncle. Saying that he'd go anywhere, he'd go to town then, leave. But he wouldn't go home again. He pictured his mother and Fran, Skip and the baby, the girls. The sound of his words echoed in his stomach, made him feel sick as he bent his head in the church in the sun so that no one would see his tears.

Thursday, September 8th. Province House, Charlottetown

ON THE LAST EVENING OF THE CANADIANS, Mercy walked into the Assembly Room that was transformed by candlelight and tables spread with white cloths. Everyone was coming to this last dinner. Coming now, not because it was the end but because they knew it was the start of something big. Now they wanted to be a part of what was happening, a part of the party. All the men coming home late, feeling young again, their lives thrumming in them in the early hours of the morning when life began to move in them. It was the grand finale — and the beginning, a feeling of anticipation, of change wafted through the air, gripped the whole island. The parade of the farmers a lark, like the circus, events meant only to entertain. No harm done, no harm meant. Everyone, everything, in high spirits. This was the talk of the men in the early morning to their wives and more soberly at lunch with their families. The coming of the new, the changing, and Mercy could hear it around her now, hear it in the women speaking with their husbands, in the tones of voice, in the lightness of the air.

This last was the grandest ball yet and Mercy watched for John A. Macdonald. She hadn't spoken with him, nor he with her since the afternoon in the widow's walk. They'd seen each other and made sure to look away. Tonight the end now, and Mercy wanted to see him. She glanced at herself in the mirror in the hall. Her orange dress, her pearls around her neck. Mr. Bernard, arriving at the same time, took her arm and she stepped forward into the room, teasing him about nothing as he laughed with her, the two of them merry, bright. She knew Macdonald would be there, knew they would dance, the end of their stay, the start of something too.

She and Bernard bowed to each other and danced this first dance together. He made her laugh with his small talk, his niceties. The floor was so crowded they were forced to dance in place caught in a corner of the room. She was about to ask Bernard about Macdonald when she looked up and saw him almost right in front of her, Macdonald and his partner caught too.

They were face to face, she and Macdonald across their partners. He looked at her and nodded, smiled. Now, the end, this final evening. He could see their reflection in a mirror on the wall. He looked at himself and almost thought to let go of his partner, raise his arm and tap the other man's shoulder, exchange partners. But the dance moved on and Mercy turned away from him, her fingers raised in a small wave.

Mercy felt the space between them, the air physical on her arm, pulling at her. She wanted to reach out, touch his shoulder, an effort of will to hold her arm still. Impossible to stay dancing there so long. She raised her hand just as Bernard turned her in the other direction and they moved away. Macdonald left where he was as the other dancers eddied past, Macdonald and his partner left behind.

And still they didn't speak. Dinner was served late into the evening and then the men began their speeches. Talking and talking, till Mercy couldn't hold her eyes open any longer. Three in the morning before she and her mother rose to leave. Macdonald stood when he saw them, tipsy, bowing low, a merry sweep of his hat toward them, "Till Quebec!" Feeling suddenly like a promise to himself, the thrill of a secret exposed.

Mercy curtsied and bowed at the same time with a wave of her hand like his. The adventure of leaving, the possibility of more suddenly there.

At four in the morning John A slapped Coles on the shoulder and said his goodbyes. The Canadians gathered together and stepped out into the cool thickness of late night. Fog all around them as they rode down to the harbour and crossed to the *Victoria*. Faint half moon making the night sleepy, the men joking and laughing, the small boat rocking tipsy together. John A happy and drunk, the conviviality of men, so pleasantly heavy in his body, relaxed, the talks over, the night over, to bed to sleep, rocked on this lullaby of water. He laughed, slapped his knee. And looking down he saw on his trousers dust of red dirt, red island clay on every piece of clothing he'd worn. He brushed at his leg and then reached over the side of the boat and gathered a handful of water. The smooth feel of salt water against his skin, the most he'd touched, realizing he hadn't swum as he'd promised.

He took off his hat and splashed the water over his head, soaking his hair and face, a christening of island salt water. Salt on his lip as he thought of Mercy Coles. A smile and a longing. How he'd danced so close beside her, how he could have reached out and changed partners, fallen in love, or proven he wasn't. And done neither. Now the salt of the water stung his lips, his tongue. He wanted the feel of a mouth on his, the taste of another, felt the pulse of his body and wanted to lose himself, needed someone. He looked up as McGee spoke.

"Aay, John, is it not as pretty a picture as I told you? Really prettier in person, simple beauty like no other. But enough of that. We're off now, back to home and our mainland beauties, our own beds waiting for us. A toast to us!"

Macdonald took the flask McGee offered him and drank, erasing the taste of salt, and he drank again. Salt water still on his face and he wiped his eyes. Yes, a toast, he raised the flask, his back turned to the island, and faced the men. Yes, yes, all of them raised their arms, all longing, believing for a moment that in their beds their lover waited. All reached, as Macdonald had done, into the sea, wanting the time, the feeling of possibility, of change not to end, here now, wanting. Each with a handful of water, his arm raised, pouring the water over his head.

Two

"The stars make no noise.
You can't hinder the wind from blowing."
       — Carl Sandberg *The People, Yes* 107

" . . . *all matters relating to intercolonial trade,*
commerce and military defences — railways and
maritime steam communication — light houses,
currency, and postal relations — emigration — settle-
ment of wild lands — land tenures, when they possess a
provincial character as they do here — uniformity in the
system of education — all these things would come under
the supervision of the Confederate Legislature, and the
then so-called Colonial Minister in Downing Street
would have no more right to interfere with our mode of
managing them than the man in the moon."
   — Edward Whelan, *Examiner* September 9th, 1864

September 4th. The circus travels to Quebec

ALEX AND THE CIRCUS LEFT SHEDIAC TWO days later. They caught another ship, travelled north up the coast of New Brunswick: Cap-des-Caissie, St. Edouard de Kent, Richibucto. Like Shediac, French and foreign to the circus, and Alex, who had stolen aboard, was put to use. He spoke French for the circus.

He used his grandmother's tongue, his father's mother Anne from the Cape Breton shore, from the 'other side' — across from Prince Edward Island. She was known for her dark beauty and because she was French. She'd lived with them when Alex was small and it had been his job to look after her. Now he spoke for the circus in this old language, its shape almost forgotten in his mouth. And all the French took on the air of his grandmother to him. The men and women, even the children holding a waft of tobacco smoke in their hair which was dark, all dark, the same as his grandmother's, and as his own.

One week later Alex and the circus were in Tracadie where the water was warm, part of the Gulf stream that circled the Island's north shore, Alex's shore. Then on to Caraquet at the mouth of the Baie des Chaleurs. By September 17th they had travelled into the mouth, Jonah swallowed, and played in Dalhousie, both port and beginning of their inland crossing of the Gaspe Peninsula. The circus was headed across the peninsula to the St. Lawrence.

This is how the circus had always travelled, Alex learned, by water. It stopped up and down the Eastern seaboard of the United States, but it had become too dangerous, warships and war the only diversions there now. And so the circus was making its first tour of the waters to the north, the great lakes and rivers of the Canadas. And Alex with them, headed for Niagara Falls.

Thursday, September 8th. Return to Quebec

THE *QUEEN VICTORIA*, WITH JOHN A AND all of the delegates, followed the circus' wake, travelling back the way it had come, heading for Quebec. At five in the morning, after the final ball on Thursday, September 8th, the delegates had boarded the *Victoria* as befogged as the harbour. They headed for Halifax, Moncton, St. John, banquets, toasts and speeches all the way up the St. Lawrence back to Quebec. John A talking till he heard himself in the middle of the night, in the middle of his dreams, his own voice waking him.

They reached the St. Lawrence, the salt tide river where pods of whales headed north, swam inland up the Saguenay, and the river ran them back out again into the sea. Tadoussac and Baie Saint Catherine, sister towns on opposite shores. John A looked out on the forests of the north shore thick with fall flowers and the mud of La Malbaie a lure, the smell of trapped sea, a stink in all of their noses. Till they reached, finally, Quebec, sitting in the sun on its hill above the river. The *Victoria* with John A and the others continued on, like the river, to Montreal, and then to Ottawa, home of the new capital, and new home for them all, the parliament building rising almost out of the locks above the canal, beside the river. The river continuing on, reaching finally the Great Lakes like inland seas, the water in a sea drift falling over itself at Niagara, to get to the river, to return to the sea. Spectators lining the shore, watching for a fall.

Alex and the circus, the famous tightrope walker Farini and the delegates, all heading for Niagara Falls.

Wednesday, October 5th. Train to St. John

MERCY FACED THE BACK OF THE TRAIN across from Mrs. Alexander. It was easier on her stomach that way, watching the land they had already passed through, seeing it as they left it behind. She traced their path away from the island. The trees here were so thick, the scenery so unchanging, it was hard to see they were moving at all. Impossible to believe in the sea here, the morning long gone and impossible too. Seasick as she'd crossed the strait, such a short span of water, only the strait. They'd left at three that morning, the fog thick and cold and she hadn't been able to see the island as they'd left the mouth of the harbour.

Now they were travelling in the wrong direction, away from Quebec, in a diagonal path to St. John. There they'd travel south down the Bay of Fundy and then take another train across the eastern states and arrive at Quebec from the other side. Never having seen the Canadas at all. And they would arrive early, before all the others who would travel on the *Queen Victoria* that the Canadians were sending.

She sighed. A party pre-empted in lieu of the journey, but she wanted the party. Just a small group of them now, her father had said he needed to be there before the others, that there was work to be done. But she knew it was the water he didn't want, on a ship for days, with the water below him deep, pulling at him. She shifted in her seat, closed her eyes. Seasick or not she would have preferred the sea. They could travel the whole way by water, leave the island by boat and continue all the way there. As though home were right there with them then, if they came by water. And they would see the mainland made visible. She'd be prepared then.

For what? The thought rose unbidden. She was ready. Four weeks of waiting, four weeks of preparations, dresses made, letters sent to the relatives in Boston and Chicago. Four weeks. She was twenty-six years old. She was more than ready.

"You can't be an islander if you can't take the sea," Mrs. Alexander said and smiled at Mercy. She waved her hand at the scene out the window, continued, "Otherwise the island becomes all there is. No different than the mainland, no different than a mainlander." Mrs. Alexander looked out, saw only trees, her own reflection. Happy to be on this trip, to be away. Possibilities, you never knew, here, now potential for a new life. The world beyond the island opening up. She looked back at Mercy, teasing her, "Because you can't have one without the other, you know." Raising first one hand, "Water," and then the other, "Or island."

Leaving Mercy to imagine herself then not what she was, not red island. And if not, then what was she? Facing backwards and suddenly lost on this trip away from home, the train disappeared in the sea of trees, overgrown wild flowers obscuring their tracks. Mercy adrift, the island gone and invisible, and her stomach sick again. Neither land nor water felt right.

She leaned back into her seat and felt the pull of the train on her back. It reminded her of the last evening of the Canadians, how the air had pulled at her when she'd danced away from John A. Macdonald. She knowing that she'd wanted to be pulled and how she'd resisted, held herself back when she wanted to go forward, reach out and touch him, and had stopped herself. Drops of a sun shower fell across the window. She raised her hand to the glass, the rain fell away from her, pulled back by the train moving forward. And she with her back turned, seeing only what was behind. Four weeks, the train speeded up, pulled her harder. She was ready. She wanted to see, wanted to go. She stood and sat beside Mrs. Alexander, faced forward watching the rain drops fall towards her.

In St. John they picked up Leonard Tilley and continued by boat again, moving down the Bay of Fundy, headed for Portland, Maine. Mercy stood on the deck and watched as they left. All there was to see was rock and water and trees. The water was high but the tide had turned and was going back out. It was the best time to leave. They'd waited at the hotel all morning for this, the high tide. Late the night before, her father had gone down to the wharf. All the water gone, he'd said at breakfast, the whole dock right down to the sea bottom, in view. The water pulled away, the boats stranded in the mud below and not a drop of water left. Strange tides that were so complete, that took everything, she thought. Not happy with some, needing it all. But why not? Why not all? She could agree with that.

Twenty-four more hours by ship. A full day and night yet. It would take that long because of the tide that pushed against them while they tried to move down the Bay of Fundy, sailing south, to get to Portland, to the train again, and the tide rising high and hard against them, trying to keep them from going. But she was going.

As they left Mercy stood beside her father who leaned over the edge of the ship. "The tides here are the highest and fastest in the world." He turned, leaned back on the rail behind him and looked up. "All because of the moon."

"Pa," she said, and took his arm to move away.

He looked back at the water. "And invisible. Except for the changing of the water itself." He reached his arm down as though he could trail it through the water far below. "Rip tides," he said then. "We have rip tides. The pull created by banks of sand under the water." He looked out at the horizon. Mercy crossed her arms and leaned against the rail with him. Nova Scotia hidden the same as the mainland, always only the shore she was on visible.

Coles leaned over the rail and looked down. He watched the green wake as the ship began to move. The lovely curve of it, the crest of white. No colour of sea better than that of the deep green below you, fresh washed wake. He wished he could touch it. "No islander should be fool enough to play with water," he said, in a soft tone, so low she could barely hear it. Something he'd once heard. Where? Who? And then he laughed and stood up away from the rail. Mercy turned to look at him. "Don't be ridiculous," he continued. "You know better than that of course. I taught you well. My own best swimmer. Just like me."

Mercy's stomach rolled, seasick before they barely left the dock. She held tight to the rail and turned away from him. Just an island girl, trapped, only knowing the whole of small. Just like him.

⚓

ALEX SPENT HIS DAYS WITH THE BROTHERS learning to balance. As their fishing boat displaced water, his body now displaced air; it was the same process.

"Ground yourself," Ben would say. "Find your feet." And then they would take turns rolling in against one another's bodies. Find the spot on the body held tight against the air. There Alex would let himself expand. His back, his shoulder, his side flowed as if water into the space of the other, the flow of his body pushing the other aside. Only a wake of air remained where the other had been. "You must know space, understand air. Where it flows, finds its stasis, where it rests," Ben said. "To count on air you must know where it lies, where it hides. Deception is misunderstanding on your part. Uncover and discover air, know how it pulls and how it holds if you don't want to be deceived by air."

Next, Alex learned how to keep the balance between them. A continual shifting, one against the other, a moving point of balance. Like the flow of water against itself, wave and sea separating and joining, losing themselves in each other. When his mind took note, became conscious of the shift, he would hesitate, the movement and momentum broken, the balance lost and they would both fall.

Ben strung lines for him, slack ropes and tightropes at angles sloping up to a tree and low across the ground. He told him to ignore the ground, whether it was close or far. To walk was to walk, and to fall was to fall. The one had nothing to do with the other. Think only of the feel of your feet, he said, the feel of the air. The secret was knowing how to adjust to the space around you. And the ground had nothing to do with it.

October 8th. Arrival in Quebec

Two days after leaving Portland, Mercy and the others boarded a special train sent for them. The regular train had moved so slowly and taken so long it seemed to Mercy they would never reach Quebec. She longed for the water even more, wanted to be travelling on the ship with the others. Here the land stretched on and on and as much as she'd imagined it, she found it hard to believe this vastness was possible.

Mercy smiled at the thought of Leonard Tilley, the only single man with five single women having to help them all admire the views. Together they had looked out at the White Mountains of New Hampshire and she had enjoyed them. The first mountains she'd ever seen. Land that not only spread wide, but rose too. Her island a flat smudge, a puddle of land caught in the sea.

Finally, at five thirty in the afternoon, four full days since they'd left Prince Edward Island, they came into Port Levis flying, half an hour early and no one there to meet them. It was pouring and almost impossible to see Quebec on the other side of the river bluing in the twilight and the dark of the rain. They left the train and got into carriages to take them down to the river to cross to Quebec. Mercy watched out the window blurred with water. The path was so steep and muddy that she was afraid the horses would slip and they would fall straight down into the river. They'd left by water and arrived by water, the strait and now this river, and here finally was the Canadas. Really, they had been travelling the south shore of Quebec for the past few hours but it was only now, only as they reached the river that Mercy thought, yes, here we are, now we are about to arrive.

On the ferry it was raining so hard that no one got out, so dark they couldn't see how the city rose up and up from the river until they left the boat and the horses had to climb through steep cobbled streets, slipperier than the mud. They stopped at the Hotel St. Louis across from a park and Mercy could see the leaves of the trees drip with the wet. Inside, she flushed from the suddenness of the heat and her head felt dizzy, the floor below her swaying as if she were still on the train. She was hardly in the door before D'Arcy McGee, George Brown, Mr. Cartier and John A. Macdonald came through from the drawing room to greet them. Everyone was laughing and loud as they shook hands, the men taking the women's hands, and Mercy waited for John A. There was a pause before he stepped forward to greet her, his hair even longer, curling and damp on his forehead.

"You are here at last," he said. As though she'd promised to come before and now was late. He continued to hold her hand, remembered the island. "Sadly, we haven't your weather to offer you." He paused, wondered when fall had turned to rain? He'd been so busy these past weeks. Had he even answered his son's letter yet? How long ago was that? He was lost in thought, forgot he held on to Mercy's hand.

"Yes, here," she looked away from him, could see the room reflected in the mirror over the fireplace, could see herself. Looking no different, and travelled so far. She looked at him again, and he bowed, let go of her hand. "We've heard so much about your Canadas," a slight stress on the 'your', "and now we will see it. See if all you say is true."

John A laughed. "I hope we live up to your expectations." He felt a lightness come over him. He'd worked hard the past four weeks, had not even gone home to see Hugh John. There would be time soon though, when these meetings were through. It would be good. And in the summer, perhaps in the summer, the island had been so beautiful, they could go together, bathe in the warmth of the sea there. "Though really, land can never compare to an island. Complete and full, its beauty enhanced by never knowing for sure when it will end." He thought of the sand that drifted out to the sea, the ease of it, how it went on, just continued. Water and sand, one with the other, endless and unending. To be there forever and watch the pull of that motion and know that nothing could make a difference. There was an easing in his shoulders.

"You say that as though you could be taken by surprise, fall off the end of the earth, like Christopher Columbus, Mr. Macdonald." She tilted her head. "Is our island as mysterious as that?" She saw herself in the mirror again, cheeks flushed against the cream skin of her face, strands of her hair curled with the rain fallen loose on her neck. Beautiful in the way one was beautiful in private. Knowing this is what he saw. And thinking I am here. Here is the world beyond the island, here is more. I am here, and now it will begin. And smelling the food for dinner coming from the far room, she felt hungry, starving even, could barely wait. She nodded her head at Macdonald, raised her arm to take his, and Mercy and John A led the way to dinner.

While they ate everyone was noisy and gay. All of them laughed at McGee's story of how the tightrope walker Farini had offered to wheel Governor General Monck across Momorency Falls, blindfolded. And how Monck had agreed as long as Brown here checked the rope and Cartier tied the blindfold. And Mercy imagined herself standing on the line above the falls, pictured the land as it would look from high atop the rope. How the river would stretch behind them, reach back all the way to the island. Seeing the island as it floated in the sea at the end of the river, as if she could see the whole of it, in plain view, right there in front of her.

SNOW BEGAN TO FALL IN THE EVENING as Macdonald rode home in his carriage and he watched out the window imagining Farini and his unlikely line above the fall of water. When he got out of the carriage he raised his head to look up at the sky, the snow falling on his face, his mouth. The first snow, and he opened his mouth like a child, wanting to believe, trusting. Catching a flake on his tongue. It melted, disappeared in his mouth, tasted of nothing, as if he had not opened his mouth, as if the snow did not exist. John A looked down. He reached his door and stepped inside, the snow on his coat melting, turning into water. A drop falling onto the floor beneath his coat, and he did not see any of it.

Water to river to sea, tears, water within and without, the pool of water that forms in a baby's head, the future of water, and John A unknowing.

THE CLOUDS ROLLED IN DIRTY ABOVE THE fields. They came from the east, the wind blowing west across the sea and inland. Moving closer as if taken by surprise by the land that suddenly appeared out of the sea. Bending down to see better, the clouds dropped seeds of water on the men and children working. All across the island the clouds slanted light and rain over the people in the fields digging potatoes in the clay. Raindrops too, on the faces of the band of men who were coming on the road from town, headed east into the wind.

Reggie was digging potatoes. He worked with his uncles and cousins. Even the small boys and girls were home from school to help. He straightened as he felt the drops of rain. Looked up at the sky and held out his hand. Just a shower. He looked down at his hand rusted red with the earth, a rivulet running a clean line across his palm. The opposite of fishing, red cut line along his palm.

Because he was standing, Reggie was the first to hear the horns. They blew hard against the east wind. The sound came in a small gust, barely audible, possible to mistake it for the call of a seabird, or a high whistle of wind through the firs. But it was field horns, he knew, coming from the north and west of them. The horns of the farmers up by the shore road that warned of the approach of the rent collectors. He called to his uncles who stood too. All of them stopped, listened. The children dug and played, and didn't notice or heed the sudden tension of their fathers around them.

The men harnessed the horses and Reggie helped attach the wagon. They got ready quickly, worried they'd be too late and followed the direction of the horns. They went north up the farm road, past the white house, the old horse in the yard. This was Reggie's first time to stand against the rent collectors.

As they hurried past the yard he smelled the last of the year's clover in the wet of the rain and he took a deep breath. His shoulders relaxed and his arms swung as he walked. He would be there to stand strong for their land. More than his father.

Close to the head of the road it was clear that the horns called from the west, about a mile away. The collectors must be headed for the shore road, to the farms flung out along St. Peter's lake. The road he'd gone on everyday to fish, the road home.

Finally Reggie could see the farmers gathered where the town and the shore roads met and he walked faster, leaned forward in his hurry. He could almost see his house through the group of farmers. Craning his head, he was able to see the front step, the side porch hidden from view by the lilac tree grown large. He moved to the side of the group, wanting to see. As if he'd forgotten why they'd come, as if he didn't see the farmers who blocked the road. He and his cousins coming for a visit. Jam and biscuits laid out in the parlour for them all and he helping his mother in the pantry put on the tea. They'd sit in the parlour, open the front door hardly ever used and spill out on to the front step. A warm day with tea steaming the windows, laughing and joking. He'd tease Fran and swing Skip through his legs. Alex would come downstairs, giving a small whoop as he jumped the last two steps as he always did.

Reggie's stomach tensed, his steps slowed. He could see the house clearly, the doors closed and no one in the yard. No one at all and Alex still gone. They reached the blockade of farmers who shifted and made room for Reggie and his uncles to join them. Unable to see the house anymore through the group of farmers, Reggie turned to face the road. A knot in his stomach at the sight of the men who came towards them, less than a quarter of a mile away. At least twenty men in uniforms of blue, all dressed the same, without hesitation, without pause, moved up the road. Here he was and here was home and no one knew, no one watched, no one who would come for him. And the rent collectors came on, marching towards them. Reggie raised his arms and shouted with the farmers. But all the while he wanted to turn and go, the house not fifty feet behind him, a month since he'd been home.

Sunday, October 9th. Hotel St. Louis, Quebec City

IN THE MORNING WHEN SHE STOOD UP out of bed, waking after four days of travelling, Mercy felt odd, her body unused to the stillness of the earth, her head dizzy again like the night before when they'd arrived. Looking outside her window, she was surprised to find the world fallen asleep under a heavy blanket of snow. It was so bright now, the sun made it hard to see against the glare and she closed her eyes and it was as though she were on the train, the floor swaying beneath her. She felt off balance, not herself, and she liked it. She looked out the window again and winter shone suddenly with sun like summer. Everything new and different. Feeling breathless, she went down to breakfast, hurrying and nearly tripped on the last step. She grabbed the rail, catching herself, laughing, carefree, heedless, new.

For Sunday Mass they went to the Cathedral, so full with people and organ music through the air that her body felt the same: reverberating, trembling. Afterwards, before returning for lunch, they toured the city. First, the Plains of Abraham, spread broad and flat, covered in white. They stopped at

Wolfe's monument, snow falling on his face. Pennies of snow over his eyes, his fate hidden from him.

Below the Plains, they drove through the gardens, the last of the flowers bending under snow, leaves that had only begun to turn, before their time. The grass yet green, as if the spring were coming, the year to begin anew. The world reversing itself. They stopped and Mercy got out of the carriage. She leaned down to see a flower. Its petals bleeding through the snow, beautiful and awry, caught there, in the midst of bloom, in the midst of snow. Like a marker for them, to place them, as the snow began to fall again and the world was white above and below. There was no trace of where they had been, just this flower she'd uncovered. And with a sudden motion, she bent down and pulled the bloom from its stalk. Only a smudged line of snow was visible where the flower had been. An anchor lifted from the sea, let loose. And her too.

They could not drive through the cemetery, the trees too thick with snow and Mercy wondered whether the island too was covered, the world erased and invisible. Anything was possible now, the world before gone and everything, really, was new. The island gone from her as she was gone from it, elation mixed with a tug of anxiety at the back of her mind, that she might not be the only one to leave. Thinking not can one ever really leave home, but, is it home that abandons the one who leaves?

ON THE ISLAND CITY OF MONTREAL, IN the middle of the St. Lawrence, the half-salt river running round it, Alex stood atop the trapeze. He reached for the bar Henry pulled over to him. Alex has done some of this before. He has swung out while seated. He has held on with his arms only, let his body trail out behind him, his legs pulled up, scooping the air and pushing it backwards. He'd swung like that, too. Now, for the first time, Ben will swing up from the other side, and Alex will let go. Enter the space between them, Alex held by the air alone. His body slight but strong, his shoulders and legs strong from swimming. Perfect for the trapeze, a lucky find for the brothers, a boy so brave.

Ben took the bar on the other side. Will was there beside Ben, Henry beside Alex. Ben gave the bar a magnificent tug and swung out far into the middle where Alex would be. He pulled his legs up on the return, seated himself. He swung forward twice, then turned himself around so when he swung upside down he would still face Alex. Ben could do this backwards too, catch someone from behind. But Alex was a beginner. Still moving forward, as though moving forward were the only way to get anywhere.

Alex wiped the palms of his hands. He'd watched this many times before. He was ready. He reached with his left hand for the bar and tugged at it so that he'd have a good grip. The air was blowing cool on his face as Alex looked out at the open space of the tent. Now, it was now. He took a breath, smiled and then stepped out. In that first moment he felt the air pass him, the pull of the ground below. He fought against it, swung his legs to go higher, and held tight to the bar. The air rippled along the hair on his arms and bare legs, the texture of skin on air, making him aware of the muscles that pulled along his side. Pushing up and out, moving him forward and back. Like a fish, like swimming. Muscles not used for the earth, but for moving through space.

Looking down, Alex saw Ben swinging upside down now. They nearly reached each other in the middle except that Ben was below him. On Alex's nod Ben will lower his arms and swing, his arms extended. Alex, reaching the lowest point on his swing out, passing the mid-point and rising again, will count to three as he's been told. Count to three and let go.

Alex nodded. He swung back once more and saw Ben lower his arms. Alex was on the way out again, was past the mid-point, on his way up. Ben, out of sight now, swung below him. Alex counted one, two, three. And let go of the bar. Entered the space that the two of them created, reaching forward, his arms outstretched, falling.

Wednesday, October 12th. Quebec City

THE SNOW TURNED TO RAIN. RAIN AGAIN, and more rain. They'd toured the city on Monday and Tuesday and now Mercy and her mother and Miss McDougal travelled out of town away from the drear of the city. Colonel Gray of PEI was chaperone of the party, and Mr. Caruthers, Mr. Galt's secretary rode in their carriage. They went to the falls of Lorette, the path so slick and wet they didn't walk down into the gorge but stood on the bridge and looked from a distance. Through the rain and the slants of snow left on the rocks Mercy saw a rainbow, like spring or summer again, but not winter.

From there they went to the Indian Chief's house, not at all what she'd expected. The last of the Huron tribe, his wife ninety years old, the two rocking in their chairs, and the children all dead. Two silver armlets from George IV and a medal from the Prince of Wales taken from an ornate wooden box, a tomahawk and the Chief's cap was all there was to show for it.

And now, idle people, her, walking through their house, and no one left to wear the armlets or the cap, no chest on which to pin the medal. When the two, father and mother, died, it would all be over, idle trinkets hanging on the wall, in the box. Leaving Mercy to feel foolish, a wooden spoon bought as a curiosity in her hand.

REGGIE AND THE FARMERS MOVED CLOSER TOGETHER. All of them watched the rent collectors as they marched forward with such straight ahead and unhurried motion as if they felt no need to gather speed, had no need of momentum. As if there were nothing in their way, no one there. The farmers felt invisible and Reggie heard them begin to mutter. This was not the way it usually happened. When the collectors found a group of farmers they made a pretence of getting past, asked to be let through, asked for the farmer they wanted. And then the collectors would turn back, all islanders, brothers. But now the collectors moved forward, did not speak, did not call out, continued towards the farmers as if they didn't see them at all.

The fathers told the boys to stay back, to get by the wagon. Reggie's neck was hunched with fear. He could feel the men around him begin to move back, give way. Like the movement of the water beneath their fishing boat, so small a movement, such a slight change and yet his stomach knew, his head felt the shift. A tinge of nausea, seasick amongst the farmers on land. When they needed to stand strong, move forward as one. But they didn't. Reggie looked around. He thought the farmers must all feel it, must all be able to tell they were being shifted, were coming apart. The collectors moved forward. Reggie pushed back to the wagon. Something had to be done. He did not want to be washed under by this wave of men. The farmers must ride over it same as the sea. They must stand close together, and not fall, not let the space between them open like a ship torn asunder.

He pulled himself up into the wagon as it moved beneath him, rolling as the men and the boys moved back again. Reggie worked to keep his balance and stand, felt afraid above the ground. He needed to shout, be heard, break the spell of the collectors, make the other men see. He stood, almost holding his breath, afraid of falling. The collectors no more than ten steps away now. And then he saw Skip running towards him from the house, rushing to Reggie who he could see standing in the wagon. Skip not paying any attention to the farmers or the collectors. Not knowing the seriousness of it. He was just a small boy, one who wanted his brother. And Reggie could see that Skip would be trapped, trampled beneath the men. No one aside from Reggie on the wagon noticed the little boy. Reggie, who'd been wishing for someone to see him, for someone to come. And now here was Skip.

Reggie wanted to stop it, stop Skip. He opened his mouth, was not even watching the collectors anymore, saw his brother disappear into the group of men. The wagon beneath Reggie suddenly released, swayed, unbalancing him. Reggie fell forward, reaching out for something to grab on to, for someone to stop his fall.

Friday, October 14th. Quebec City

I T   W A S   R A I N I N G   S T I L L ,   A N D   S H E   H A D   a sore throat.

In order to get outside, Mercy and her mother took their umbrellas and went for a walk along Durham Terrace. They walked past the park, going uphill where the land tilted up and away from the river. To their left the town sloped down, the streets circling round to reach the lower town and then the river, and on their right was the Plains of Abraham, the fortress and the wall. Durham terrace was a broad rock promenade above the lower town and they walked towards the far end of it where they could look out over the river and Levi on the other shore. The rain drizzled, the air more damp than real rain and a few other couples strolled along the terrace. A family with the small boys pulling at their father's hands walked ahead of them, and Mercy thought of Russell at home, missing them, missing her father. The afternoon light was weak, the clouds blooming brown above the river as she put her umbrella down, the air against her face, like an afternoon at home, sea damp air without the salt.

Behind them suddenly there was a loud crashing sound and a tremor beneath their feet. Everyone turned, and Mercy and her mother and all the others hurried back along the terrace. People were gathered at the edge just above where the Rue. St. Pierre began. A large piece of the rock cliff had fallen away into the street below, and had knocked people down as it slid past. The noise of it unexpected, shocking, the sucking sound of mud a shushing in the quiet of the rain. In the street below Mercy saw a woman in a green coat, her arms spread wide as if frozen in wonder, suddenly fall to her knees in the rock and mud. The sound of the earth shifting continued. Mercy heard the rock slipping wet against the earth sliding into the street, into the people, making them stumble as they moved out of the way. Everyone rushed from the falling slide of the earth, from the rock cliff precarious above their heads. Only the woman in her green coat was left kneeling in the mud, frantically digging at the earth and rock.

In Montreal Alex prayed the timing was right. A slight change caused by the push of the legs, an altered angle of wrist or foot, too early or too late and he would miss, the body deceived by air. The first, the only fall.

Friday, October 14th, evening. Hotel St. Louis, Quebec City

Mercy was brushing her mother's hair in front of the mirror in her parents' room. The first ball and she felt tired. Her throat was still sore. A touch of fever even, she thought. She'd slept through the afternoon after coming back from their walk and still she was tired. Her mother was dressed in dark green silk, her hair brown yet. In the light Mercy could see the powder on her mother's face, the hint of pink on her cheek. She wished for this evening they were home and she could sit curled into her mother on the sofa in front of the fire, warm flannel around her throat and her mother stroking her hair, the night outside, sea rain and wind against the windows a lullaby of warmth.

Mercy wanted to cry. She was too old to feel like this. She ran her finger over her mother's cheek and her mother looked up.

"How lucky you are. How young." She paused, reached up and touched Mercy's face. "Smile darling. Don't worry. Don't be anxious."

She glanced at Mercy and back at the box and handed a necklace of pearls to Mercy to put around her neck. Her mother's hands so warm, Mercy wanted to hold them for a moment, pull them to her face.

Her father came into the room and she jumped, startled. Saw herself in the mirror, dressed in her blue gown, her hair not done yet, her body with a slight waver in the curve of the mirror. Her face an odd blur, white, her eyes too bright. She bent to finish pinning her mother's hair and then straightened. Her father paced for a minute and then sat down by the window.

"The road is still blocked, the lower town in chaos," he said. "The rain and the mud are slowing the work of shoring up the cliff."

He looked out the window, drummed his fingers on the table beside him. Mercy's mother turned to him and Mercy looked in the mirror brushing her own hair. The sound of his fingers like the rain on the window, the rain still falling, fallen all the day, a drumming in her head. He looked back at them, impatient, revved up, her mother constantly trying to slow him down.

"Some people injured," he continued. "A baby dead."

Mercy watched herself in the mirror, pale, seeing the woman in green who had stood with her arms extended. Had she been holding a baby? And in the tumult of the air, in the surprise of the noise, had she been startled and opened her arms, the baby falling through and into the earth, into the street, the earth sliding over its small and sleeping face? Mercy shivered, gone so cold and now so hot, her legs aching. The room through the mirror tilted, slanted up at her. She closed her eyes. Opened them again, saw herself standing with the brush in her hand, the room beginning a slow spin. Heard again the crash of the rock, felt the shake of the earth. She wanted the spinning and the noise to stop but everything became louder, faster. She closed her eyes again. The only sound was that of the brush against the floor as she fell.

"Reggie," Skip called. Reggie was kneeling on the wagon, caught before he'd fallen out. He looked and there was Skip below him at the side of the wagon reaching for Reggie's hand. Skip safe and sound. Reggie looked out at the group of farmers. They stood unmoving where they'd stopped. The rent collectors stopped there too, almost touching shoulders with the farmers. Everyone was silent, surprised by the sudden stillness. The collectors shifted on their feet, embarrassed to be so close, seeing the farmer's faces scared, vulnerable with the surprise of all movement stopped. The pitchforks of the farmers hung loosely in their hands and the two groups faced each other for a moment, saying nothing.

The moment lengthened, as if neither side knew what to do. Then the farmers shook their heads, and not looking at each other, began to move forward. The rent collectors searched for each other in the crowd, anxious now, alone. They were twenty separate men, not a group any longer as each turned away and walked back down the road the way he had come.

Reggie climbed down from the wagon and took Skip's hand. He watched as the farmers began to walk down the road in slow pursuit, hesitant of their easy victory as he and Skip stood there alone. The boys from the wagon followed their fathers and Reggie and Skip just watched. Skip pulled on Reggie's hand. "Come on Reggie. Come on up to the house. Come see the chicken I caught today. On my fishing line. Fran gave me such a scolding. Come see it."

He pulled on Reggie, thinking Reggie was coming home now as the two of them began to walk up the road together. Reggie, reaching the Ryan's field, turned off the road and went up through the field, Skip walking ahead chattering back at him. Low summer blueberry bushes scratched at their legs as Reggie walked forward, wanting to see the house, say hello to his mother. Knowing his father would be away. Wanting to go in and he hurried through the field with his brother.

They reached the side yard, passed the old shed whose roof still waited to be repaired. "Now you hush, Skip. I'm just going in for a minute." They went up the step to the porch. Reggie could hear his mother in the kitchen. He put out his hand to stop Skip. He wanted to see first. He stood to the side of the summer door and looked in. Through the porch he could see his mother, her back to them making bread. She wore her pale green dress covered with the flowered apron. She was singing.

"Come see my chicken I caught Reggie. Come on now. You can talk to Ma later." Skip pulled at Reggie.

Reggie stayed by the door hidden from his mother's view. Watched her, the kneading of the bread, the song lilting lightly, her body in a dance of bread and song. He wanted to go in, touch her shoulder, surprise her. Seeing her from the back as he did on their rides to church. With her purple hat gauzy with flowers, the smell of her powder, a Sunday perfume in his nose, erasing the memory and smell of fish. He longed for her to turn around, come out to the porch and open the door, find him.

Still she sang on, did not turn around, did not come out. How could she sing without them? Without Alex, without him? She sounded so happy. He couldn't understand. He waited at the door, unnoticed, unremembered. She couldn't tell he was there, waiting for her, didn't answer. Didn't want him, prodigal son, Cain at the door.

Skip tugged at him again and Reggie pulled away. Jumped from the porch in one step, his mother turning at the sound, seeing nothing. The October sun broke through the clouds, the light beyond the screen door showed only a dance of dust over the pump.

Reggie walked fast down the field as Fran came from behind the house just then, but Reggie was already far away and didn't see her drop the laundry basket, her mouth opening. He reached the road and joined the farmers as they turned back for home. Reggie walked faster now, didn't look back, Skip left in the yard, watched his brother leave. Again.

ALEX FELL INTO THE SPACE CREATED BY the two of them, his arms reaching out and Ben ready, adjusted his swing to Alex's fall. The blur of the tent a wave like the sea, a slow pulse that buoyed Alex up. He fell, an exhilaration through him as he entered the open space flying through the air, not even water, nothing at all, holding him. Forgetting his lessons, forgetting air, the turn with his head that would extend his fall. Only Ben letting go early, sooner than planned, falling beyond his knees and holding on with his feet, a difficult trick even for Ben, saved him.

Alex caught at the last moment, saved, not even noticing it was the last moment.

Wednesday, October 19th. Hotel St. Louis, Quebec City

FROM HER BED MERCY WATCHED THE FLICKER of the shadows on the wall made by the candle on the dresser. She'd asked her mother to leave it lit when they left for the ball. Another dinner and ball she was missing. Sick since she'd arrived. She'd missed every event so far, all the banquets, the dances starting once the others had arrived on the *Victoria*. Again — if only they'd come on the *Victoria* with everyone else. Not the train, not the other boats where she must have caught diphtheria. All because of her father.

She pushed herself under the covers. God, how her throat hurt; she needed more ice. She wished her mother had stayed, wished she were back home in her own bed, Ide and Russell to get her some ice, distract her. Her head hurt, her throat so swollen tonight they'd cut it. She started to cry again thinking of the blood on Tupper's arm, her blood. Tupper's daughter had died last year, diphtheria too. She shivered. Now her. Her mother holding her hand had looked away at the sight of the knife.

Mercy turned to the wall, rested her forehead against the coolness of the headboard. She was hot, then cold. She turned again, her legs restless, in bed for days. The wine they'd given her for her throat thrummed in her head, her eyes hot and bright from it and fever and crying. She was sick of being here alone, sick of not going out, sick of being sick. On the chair by the dresser lay her new opera cloak, the red of its lining fallen open on the chair. Reflected in the mirror the candle glowed, looked warm, beckoned her.

Hot, she pulled off the covers and got out of bed. She stood on the floor in her bare feet, shivered. She should stay in bed but walked over to the dresser. In the mirror she could see her dresses hanging in the closet, like girls standing idle at the ball waiting for a dance, like she was. She picked up her opera cloak and wound it round her waist. Orange red silk lining turned to the outside, a makeshift skirt. Mercy smiled at herself in the mirror and walked backwards into the centre of the room watching herself. She did a slow turn, her head over her shoulder, and watched as long as she could. She curtsied as though there was someone else there, raised her hand and turned again in a waltz of one. She moved in a slow dance, turning, making herself dizzy.

The movement enticed her, melted away the rawness of her throat, the soreness of her joints, her skin tight with fever. She turned faster, her head beginning to spin and looked down at her skirt, burnt red like the island soil in this light. Turned rust, burnt by the air, by its nature, because it was there. She spun faster, watched the skirt flare out against the whiteness of her legs. It was like fire leaping round her, surrounding her, spinning, turning, going faster and faster. Flames lapped at the floor, rose, circled her, her eyes glazed. She watched mesmerized, her own spinning body the fire swelling, gleaming, fluttering. She was red fire, hot with fever, her heart pounding in her head. Dancing, spinning, she and the fire spinning together.

Suddenly banging up hard against the windowsill, she stopped. Mercy raised her hand to her shoulder with a cry of pain, tears in her eyes. At the window she faced out into the rain, at the gray slate roofs of the city, and the wet dark roads, the smell of mud from the river covering all. Tears ran down her face. She needed her sea. Red hot island adrift alone, stuck here in a dank river without water enough to cool it. How she missed it. What had she done, gone and left it and now here she was, the floor cold under her feet, shivering, sick. Stuck here, the river moving on past, going home without her. The island forsaking her, alone, and no one there. Oh God, please let someone come, don't let me be alone, don't let me die. She was so cold. Sobbing now, shaking with fever, great breaths that seared her throat. Delirious, she imagined the fifteen Indian children, the last of the tribe, balanced on the edge of the windowsill like the edge of rock cliff, topple down, fall over the edge. She stumbled, falling forward, salt blood and tears in her mouth as she fell unconscious at the edge of the bed.

Hallucinating in the night she dreamed of her father swimming, holding a baby up in his arms as he used to hold her on the lawn in front of the house, a balancing act held in his hand. In her delirium holding the baby in water deep over his head, treading water and slowly winding down as if he were a watch or a toy boat, his body the flesh covered mechanics, slowly sinking and the baby with him. Drowning, she was drowning, impossible to get any air, bubbles of blood came from her mouth, drowning with him, the two of them sinking. He reached out to her, took her hand, pulled her down with him as she struggled to rise, fought against the pull, fought against him. Floundering with a soundless cry, suffocating, unable to swallow, drowning.

An hour later her mother found her fallen unconscious on the floor by her bed, the fever at its peak. Mercy drenched, as though she'd been submersed in water.

THE FARMERS WALKED UP THE ROAD TOGETHER, some turning off and going back along the shore road while others continued on towards St. Peter's Bay with Reggie and his uncles. Each looked a little tired now, except for the boys in the wagon who talked loudly and excitedly. "Did you see? Yeah, and then . . . " The farmers stayed quiet, not knowing really why the collectors had stopped. Just that they had, there in front of the farmers, stopped, the collectors looking surprised, too. Each farmer knew that he'd been about to give way, was being pushed aside. Had shifted so that he wouldn't be plowed under. Afraid of the rent collectors as they had moved forward, not stopping. Each farmer knew in his soul he was to blame. Knew they had lost. That they would have failed because he had given way. But the collectors had stopped. God drumming his fingers aimlessly, an idle miracle bestowed on those who had lost faith.

No one saw Skip as he had run forward. How he had broken through, torn a line through the collectors, a break in the air that pushed them apart. No one except Reggie who had seen it at the last moment, felt the break, the wagon released from its hold, jarring free as the men stopped moving backwards. Causing him to fall forward, almost falling out of the wagon onto his head. Except that he'd been stopped, too. Someone had grabbed his arm, saved him at the last moment. But when he'd looked there'd been no one there. No one who had grasped his arm. No one had been there at all to save him.

Wednesday, October 19th. Quebec City

IN THE MIDST OF THE CONFERENCE, THE Canadians having reneged on their deal, no money to buy out the landlords, the blight on the island's rosy constitution, Ned Whelan Islander turned turncoat, against Pope, against Coles, against his own party, stirred by the law, by the democracy of it all and by the size of the Canadas, the firmness of the land, not like the island, a patch of sandbank shifting in the Gulf of St. Lawrence, said yes to union as all his fellow island delegates voted no, no, and no.

Wednesday, October 19th, evening. Quebec City

AFTER THE ISLANDERS TOOK THEMSELVES AWAY, FINISHED their separate talks, George Coles was off to the big ball. Dancing and dancing all the evening, he and Macdonald both dancing till the very end. The last to leave, the two laughed as they came out into the cool of the outside air. Happy, large, drunk, wet with perspiration, and now rain.

Macdonald said, "Give my best to your wife, and daughter, we missed them. Better now I hear. Pretty and smart, lucky man."

Macdonald giving himself a momentary pause. Too full, too bright and big to care, really, just now too busy. Ah, what a night, he thought. The rain made it all the nicer inside. Lit windows nicest in a rain and cold darkened night. To sit by the fire with a drink, fall into bed. He was a heavy sleeper. It was a wonderful thing. He thanked God for it. They both slipped as they walked through the snow melting into rain. "You'd think we were drunk," Macdonald laughed to Coles. Liking Coles, a glorious man, bigger than the others. Yes, yes the island would come along yet, practicalities to consider. Coles knew that, understood that. A man like Macdonald himself, knowing things took time.

George Coles felt as big and bright as Macdonald. Macdonald's heart worn clearly, liking people. Coles wished he were the same, not haunted by fears, not dark when he wasn't light. Coles always one or the other — lost in thoughts of failure, or driven too high, wanting more. He wanted to be liked the way Macdonald was liked, the man a sun. Barely thinking of Mercy when he answered, "Yes, better in no time," he said. As if Mercy had never been away. "Dancing, I'm sure, the night through. Wanting to catch up on all she's missed, poor girl." He himself felt lucky to be out, to be dancing, to be here and away. Not thinking of lucky for love, lucky to be held, contained. Both wet with rain and sweat as they got into the carriage. Their hands slipped from each other's grip as they said goodnight, laughing and gay, Coles sliding away.

Three

Canadian Boat Song

Faintly as tolls the evening chime
Our voices keep tune and our oars keep time.
Soon as the woods on shore look dim,
We'll sing at St. Ann's our parting hymn.

Row, brothers, row, the stream runs fast,
The rapids are near and the daylight is past.

Why should we yet our sail unfurl?
There is not a breath the blue wave to curl;
But, when the wind blows off the shore,
Oh! Sweetly we'll rest our weary oar.

Blow breezes blow, the stream runs fast,
The rapids are near and the daylight is past.

Ottawa's tide! This trembling moon
Shall see us float over thy surges soon.
Saint of this green isle! Hear our prayers,
Oh, grant us cool heavens and favouring airs.

Blow, breezes, blow, the stream runs fast,
The rapids are near and the daylight's past.

— First published in *Blackwood's Magazine*,
September 1829

October 1864. Niagara Falls, New York

AT NIAGARA FALLS, WILLIAM HUNT — FARINI, the daredevil tightrope walker from Port Hope, Ontario — stepped out of his hotel in the early morning. He glanced up at the hotel across the street and studied the room directly opposite his. It was the room that Blondin always took when he was in town. And Farini always made sure to have the hotel and the room across from Blondin's. The two high wire stunt men had never met, never acknowledged each other, but each knew everything the other did. A contest of skill, a contest of bravery, of ego. Who would win? Who would draw the biggest crowds? The contest made all the more intense by their never meeting.

Each had spurred the other on to more wild, more daring adventures every day. They walked with their feet in sacks along their lines over top of the falls. They walked blindfolded. Carried men on their backs. Sometimes both together, blindfolded and carrying a man, usually their managers, above the falls, above the whirlpool. Blondin with his stove on his line above Devil's Whirlpool, cooked an omelet, and sat on a chair in the middle of his line to eat. Farini imagined Blondin with his dainty French napkin dabbing his mouth. Farini, his line stretched almost overtop of the American Falls, had lowered himself on a long rope down to the Maid of the Mist, and climbed back up again. He sighed remembering. That had been more difficult than he'd imagined. The rope wet, making his climb slow, slipping downwards with each step up, and the climb endless.

The crowds they had drawn though, biggest when they had both been there, the sum greater than what each could pull alone. Farini's best stunt so far had been his walk in the night. He imagined what the crowds had seen, his silhouette lit by the lights he carried on each end of his pole, magic and impossible. But this stunt now, this one would top them all. Farini looked away from the hotel and shrugged his shoulders. It was four years since Blondin had been here. He wasn't here now, was not in the hotel and room opposite Farini's. He'd gone home to France years ago. Blondin hadn't known how to get the supporters Farini did, Farini the high wire business man. But Farini missed him, almost thinking, wishing, that Blondin had word somehow of this next trick, and was here, up in his usual room.

Farini couldn't help himself. He glanced back as he walked down the street toward the falls. There was no sign that Blondin was there. Besides, he'd been very careful, had not let any word of this new stunt out. Today was the first try and it was too early for anyone to see. Everyone asleep at this hour of the morning, the falls forgotten, everyone believing that while they slept the world slept too. By the time he was done, just a few people would be there, enough to raise a mystery, a clamor, create a myth. And then he would promote and perform it. Ah, he loved it here. The sound of the falls a constant, the damp always in the air making the town waver, like a funhouse mirror, a mirage in front of their eyes. The spectacle of the falls trembling, impermanent, and thus it was only the moment that mattered, the town festive in the way of transience. He loved this heightened living where only the present mattered, no future, no past, a parade of spectators passing through, wanting awe.

He and his man who was carrying a long heavy sack, reached the riverbank above the American falls, the grand horseshoe of the Canadian falls beyond hidden in its own mist. Farini looked to the right. In the early morning his line was barely visible, a slight glint, only the possibility of something in the sky that was more night than day. His line stretched from the peninsula on the other side of the American falls, reached over the river where the water flumed above the rocks, to the riverbank just below the falls. It was a quarter of a mile almost from where they stood here at the edge of the falls because this new trick did not involve his high wire. The two men looked at the river; the spray of the water took on the luster of the sun just rising. At this hour, the sun on water, always a promise, almost a prayer.

They walked along the bank silently till they came to the spot Farini had selected. There the man lay down the long bag he had been carrying. Farini took off his coat and sat to put on the shoes he had in his pack. He took out the thick gloves and then turned to the man. Yes, yes, he was ready. It was getting late and he was in a rush now. The sun seemed brighter, higher more quickly than he'd expected. From the bag on the ground Farini took what he had created especially for this trick, a pair of stilts, their tips made of steel to hold strong and steady to walk along the rocky bed of the river, in the rapids, at the top of the falls.

Wednesday, October 26th. Hotel St. Louis, Quebec City

MERCY SAT IN THE DINING ROOM, HER first time down to dinner since she'd been sick. Her head hurt. The room was loud with everyone talking and the sound of the rain against the window. It felt odd to be back, odd after being alone away sick for nearly the past two weeks. Taking a panicked gasp of air, she realized she was holding her breath, tight with fear as she remembered the pain in her throat, unable to breathe. She tried to calm herself, reassured herself that she was well. The change was too sudden and she wished for the quiet, for the dim. And now here, back, as though all were the same, though she'd nearly died. She reached for her glass, the water beading through her glove cold against her skin. John A. Macdonald sat down beside her. She did not drink but lowered her glass.

"Welcome back, Miss Coles." He nodded at her. "We've missed you."

He had not visited, though others had. She'd wondered about him. Everything had ended when it seemed about to begin. She was ready for everything to begin. And then it all stopped, nothing. She'd nearly died and it didn't seem to matter. As though alive or dead were the same. She looked away and lifted her glass, drank. It didn't matter. She had lived. Everything would continue again, as though nothing were different, as if the world could not suddenly end. All one counted on, that one expected, everything one took for granted, all just pretend, a game to be played.

It was too bright and her eyes watered. "I'll be glad to be away from Quebec," but not thinking of home, "away from

this rain." Mercy spoke with impatience, as though he were
the cause of the rain, or the rain the cause of her sickness. She
turned towards him. "Does it always rain like this in Quebec?
How can you stand it?" And looked away again. She felt
foolish, silly. She sounded like a child. It made her feel even
more aggravated.

"I don't notice it," he said, which wasn't true. He often
noticed the smell of the earth, the texture of the snow, but in a
sporadic fashion, not in a gradual way. It was as though there
of a sudden, there was snow, or rain, as though there had been
nothing there at all till he noticed it. He shrugged his shoulders, raised his glass and drank, then continued. "You should
be used to it. It seems you are always with water, one way or
another, sea or rain wherever you are." In his glass, the two of
them were reflected back at him. "An islander and water, you
can't separate them." He paused. "I never did swim." A weari-
ness drifted over him. So busy now. There had been the talks,
the swaying of men, the drinking, the dancing. He was good
at it. Loved it. And he remembered his first sight of the island
as it rocked on the waves, a lullaby of sun and rest.

She looked down at her plate. "Yes water. I can't seem to
escape it." She had dreamed over and over again while she
was ill, of drowning. Sitting in the garden or lying in bed,
water slowly rising round her. Surprising her while all the
land around her filled and swelled with water, engulfed her,
taking her under. And beneath her not sand but earth or
chair, her bed, and her clothes heavy and wet. Waking cold or
sometimes hot, her chest tight, barely breathing at all, till she
fully wakened, coughing and choking. She shivered, felt faint.

Macdonald looked away. He felt heavy, like sleep, and
wanted to be away, the weight tugging at him.

Mercy was white. She was still sick, would pass out here at the table. To stop herself, in an effort of will, her hands gripped the edge of the table and she turned to him. Any small talk would do, something to distract her, force her attention to focus, not let herself fall here. "England is an island. Aren't you from there?"

"Scotland." He looked at her. "We left when I was very young. I don't remember it." But he did remember mists over low green fields and the scratch of the hedge he'd hid in playing games with his sisters, idle memories that he hadn't remembered before. "Even your island . . . " Seeing the line of cloud over the sea from the widow's walk, and the smooth brown texture of the skin of her bare hand raised against the window. Someone used to being out of doors, uncosseted, still young. "If it's not right there in front of me . . . " He looked down at his plate, new potatoes with butter and pepper. He picked up his fork then looked at her, smiled. "Now this food I can believe. This is real."

Mercy looked away. "Well, the island is real I can assure you, whether it is here in front of us or not. I can see it plainly." But she couldn't. She couldn't remember the smell of the air, or how the clouds moved across the sky. It was gone from her and she it, as though she had died. The island sunk and gone. There was a weight across her chest; she was dizzy. What was this to him? To her? Such idle chatter.

"Steadfast, then." He continued eating. "True. You have faith."

Mercy stopped. She looked at him, shook her head. Every night she had been afraid to let herself fall, every night too anxious to sleep, and in the morning her eyes were hazed. "No, I think that is exactly what I don't have." She looked down and pointed to the food on her plate. "You're right, this is real," and she cut a piece of meat and ate it.

"Well, you can't go wrong having faith in what you see." He said this with a straight face, as though he were serious.

Mercy laughed. "I agree." She nodded. "Here I am, here is everyone, and here is this food. From now on, Mr. Macdonald, I will believe as you suggest — everything I see. And nothing that I can't see."

"Much safer. You know then what you can count on, you won't be deceived, fooled." He nodded, drank. "Now, you have the tour. Everything you wanted of the Canadas. You will see it, believe it for yourself." He swirled his hand around. "More balls, banquets. Dances, we haven't had one yet."

"Then you have forgotten the island." Seeing again the light that laced the water under the full moon, the first night, when he had spoken to her. As she'd turned away from the water remembering her father. Drowning and drowning and drowning, leaving her. Fooling them, fooling her.

Macdonald looked at her. "Miss Coles?"

Mercy looked up and then back at her plate. Picked up her fork. Always water, everywhere water. And she wanted away. "Well, we can now," she said. Meaning now that they would leave, move on from Quebec, away from the rain, move inland.

John A, in the spur of the moment, wanted to be up, moving, stood and offered her his hand.

Mercy eating, stopped and looked up at him. She did not understand at first what he was doing. And then she realized. She smiled. She stood and took his hand, curtsied with mock formality, and put her left hand against his shoulder. They nodded at each other, the two of them playing. They did a box step in place, then waltzed, moved past the tables as though side stepping couples on the dance floor. Danced in time to themselves until the musicians playing for dinner, picked up their rhythm, changed time to a waltz and kept company with them. Dancing as if it were the most natural thing in the world to dance in the midst of dinner, in the middle of eating. Until all the others stopped eating and watched Mercy and John A. And then they too turned to each other and smiled. Nodded and stood. And danced. Everyone dancing with Mercy and John A in the middle of eating, in the midst of dinner.

What Alex noticed first was the sound. They were on the edge of town, away in a field, yellow aspen leaves fluttering around their wagons in the damp mist of early morning. The air was wet with the sound of water when it is stirred up, moving, the sea in a tidal flux at full moon, the edge of a storm. Alex couldn't resist. He rose and left his spot in the wagon. He was pulled by the sound, by the feel of the air. He needed to see the falls.

When he arrived at the river Alex was unable to believe his eyes. There, almost at the edge of the falls, a man stood two feet above the water, held impossibly in place, just standing as the water crested white, splashed up at him, pulled at him. Alex could not take his eyes off the man who he could see now was on stilts. He watched him struggle and lean close to the water, pulling at the pole attached to his left leg. The man was stuck, the stilt stuck. The man pulled and pulled, and then gave up for a moment, his face white as he looked at the water and back to a man on shore. Alex felt his stomach curl, a lightness in his head, felt faint as he watched. There was no one else there, only the man at the edge of the river and the man on stilts in the water above the falls, and Alex. The man on stilts leaned forward again, his face intense as he pulled and still nothing gave way. Alex watched as the man stood up straight, stopped trying and looked towards the peninsula where he must be headed and then at the falls.

Alex listened to the sound of water, the splash of it, the unmistakable feel of it in the air. He closed his eyes. It was so long since he had been in the water. Since he'd left home, forever. He looked up quickly when he heard the man on shore shout. The man in the water was gone. Alex stared. He could see nothing, no one in the water. The river flowing on past, the man submerged, invisible. And then they saw him rise. He was fighting the water now, trying to stand in the rapids. He was free of his stilt. He must have gone under and freed his feet from the bindings. Now he used the one pole, wedged it into the ground, worked to hold himself in place. He began to inch forward slowly, anchoring himself with the stilt, his legs braced into the ground against the pull of the water as he tried to move the stilt ahead.

People began to gather at the side of the river, talking and pointing. They hadn't seen him go under, hadn't seen him as he'd stood on his stilts above the water. They watched the spectacle, the man moving through the water at the edge of the falls, as if it were a show, Alex thought. Expecting wonder, expecting surprise. Farini, they said, the tightrope walker. Alex looked at them and back at the man. He looked over at the high wire the people pointed to, the line across the air of the falls, the world a circus, the world a wonder, just as he'd imagined it, as he believed it, right here, before him, here, ready.

Farini was tiring and took even smaller steps. He stopped and stared at the falls. It was impossible. He couldn't keep going. Alex felt the pull of it in his gut, the lure, the temptation to be pulled too. Then Farini let go of his pole and fell forward into the water. Alex gasped and he and the watchers on the riverbank stepped back, a movement together, as though wary they too would be tempted into the water. He watched as Farini fought to stay above the water, saw him taken under and watched as Farini rose again for a moment, then disappeared. Alex held his breath. Impossible to believe he would see the man drown right there in front of him. Farini was gone. At the very last moment, Alex saw Farini throw his arm up, catch himself on the limb of a tree on the small rock island at the edge of the falls. He watched as Farini was stopped there, held in place as the water flowed past, and watched as Farini slowly pulled himself up, dragged himself onto the shore and lay there, face down on the island on which no man or animal had ever set foot.

WHEN THEY ALL RETURNED TO THEIR SEATS the conversation continued, a little louder, more merry. They talked of the tour ahead, of Montreal and Ottawa. Of the trip around the lake, through Kingston and Toronto and on to the Falls of Niagara. Everyone talked eagerly, looking forward to the trip. Mercy was eating new potatoes, the taste of home, the first time she'd enjoyed eating anything in the past two weeks. The two of them, Mercy and John A, still connected in the dance, a shift in one causing a change in the position of the other. A synchronicity of movement though they were turned away from each other and talked to the people beside them. Mercy felt how every subtle movement in her changed him, knowing, with an edge of thrill, that if she were to stand now and leave, he would follow.

As dinner ended they moved to the drawing room, the women first as the men lingered behind talking. Mercy sat on the blue couch by the fire, a silk cushion at her back. She felt a draft of night air come in through the window; the damp of it mixed with the smell of the wood smoke in the small room. Macdonald was the first to enter the room. He walked over to her bringing her dessert. As if he ought to do it, as if he always would do it.

He sat with the men and poured himself a drink. The talks were over, Mowat finished with his finances. Seventy-two resolutions, the draft completed. Next the tour to convince the people. He rested back into his chair. He liked the smell of damp wood, the same as the smell of night in the trees by his lake and the wet leaves of fall at home. Here it was nearly winter, rain becoming snow too soon in the season. They were headed back now, towards home. He closed his eyes for a moment, smiled. He'd stop, see Hugh John. He raised his glass, drank.

Mercy sat silent holding her plate. She wished she could take off her gloves and feel the air on her skin, the coolness of the fork against her palm, the texture of the plate. She wanted to touch, feel the air. She could feel the cushion at her back, was conscious of how her legs touched each other under her dress, and how her feet rested lightly on the floor, every inch of skin aware, everything magnified. She watched a drift of smoke rise to the ceiling, the air quivering in the damp. She sat eating her cake. There was a crumb at the corner of her mouth. Raising her hand, she dusted the crumb away, leaving lemon sugar on her lip. She licked it away, a small indelicacy, her napkin held in her hand. And she saw Macdonald look up at her just then, but her small tongue was out of her mouth.

John A watching, smiled as he looked away, the tip of her tongue sweet in her mouth.

ALL THE DAY LONG ALEX STAYED BY the side of the river. Others came and went, wondered how the man had gotten there, sitting so incongruously, so impossibly on the island at the edge of the falls. Alex let the others talk, heard them as they chatted. Some said he'd fallen off his high wire and been blown to the island in his fall. Some that he'd swum to the island, fighting the current all the way, until he'd tired out and given up, let the water take him, and was saved anyway. Others, scoffed at by the rest, said they'd seen him swimming as if at the shore, taking his time and he'd stopped there merely to have a rest. All day Farini sat there with his head bowed and didn't look up at the people on the riverbank. He stood only once and paced the island. There was no way off the island, no way back to shore. He'd been saved, had saved himself. But with no way to return, saved was not saved at all, thought Alex.

Late in the afternoon, movement and noise came from the back of the on-lookers. Someone was trying to push his way through to the front, and the people around Alex pushed back until a man called out to make room, saying that it was Farini's brother. The people parted in hushed tones, and pushed forward again in curiosity to watch him. He passed right by Alex who could see the look of excitement and anticipation on the man's face. The man hurried through, moved so close to the water's edge barely watching his step so that he nearly slipped and just stopped himself from falling in. He waved his arms at Farini who sat slumped, not paying attention to the crowd. The man waved and called, till finally, either Farini caught a fragment of the man's voice, or he just happened to look up, Alex wasn't sure which. But Farini looked up and stared at the man and then sat up straight. He raised his hand to shield his eyes from the glare of the water and stood quickly. He walked to the edge of his island and when he got there he gave a whoop. Alex heard the echo of it come to him over the water. Farini waved back and the two men, grins on their faces, waved at each other as if any moment they would reach out and grasp each other's proffered hands, a handshake or a hug, no water between them, as if one were not about to go over the falls.

The brother sat down at the side of the river, opened the basket he had been carrying and took out a sandwich. He ate as he stared over at the island, raised his hand and waved his sandwich at his brother, like a toast and a salute, Alex thought. Farini too, sat at the edge of his island and waved back at his brother. The crowd waited and when nothing more happened it seemed to shrink, lose air, disappointed by the lack of fanfare. People began to drift away but Alex stayed, waiting, expecting something, he didn't know what. He watched the two brothers sitting watching each other, into the dusk of the evening, the coolness of the breeze picking up. Finally Alex rose, the last to leave, the man already having pulled out a blanket by the river's edge. Alex wandered off, avoiding the circus, too late now, into the town for something to eat, someplace to stay. He lay down at the edge of a barn; a feeling of loneliness settled over him, permeated his sleep. A boy with so many brothers and sisters, never alone, always wanting more. Wanting to see, wanting to know, around the corner, to the end of the trees, the curve of the dunes always walking further, to see beyond. Believing in more, something there, waiting for him — if he could reach it, if he could find it. And always someone waiting, watching for him.

REGGIE WALKED ACROSS THE FIELD, HIS FEET rolling, unsteady. Pine cones filled the tilled lines at the edge where he walked. He stretched his arms and yawned, put his hands in his pockets, the afternoon cool and damp. He wanted a little air before the Sunday dinner. Thinking of the dance last evening as he walked through the windbreak of trees. Bending his head, the branches low, chickadees above him called, a prayer for food. He hadn't brought anything with him. He looked into the field. Old bits of corn, leaves of summer vegetables fallen brown and left behind. Like the debris behind their fishing boat, the sea strewn with the waste that followed the boat. Nothing for them here. He shrugged his shoulders at them. "Come winter, come winter, I'll make sure I have something for you."

The old orchard was at the back of the fields. It was left to run wild, the branches unpruned reaching up and out. Reggie liked it in there. It was quiet except for the birds, time there stopped, the trees grown tall around it, the orchard hidden from view. Unpicked, the crabapples dried on the tree, rust red balls blooming in fall. Falling underfoot too, the air smelling sweet with them. Reggie picked one from the tree and pressed it between his fingers. He held out his hand, a chickadee lighting. Red etching of crabapple left in his palm. He ran his finger over it, tasted it. Cold and sweet, fermented on the tree.

He put his hands back in his pockets, looked up at the sky. Why had he gone to the dance? He knew his father would be playing. Why hadn't he let it be and stayed home, he and Mary Beth going out for a walk, playing cards? But he'd wanted the music and the dance, wanted the lights. His cousins going. Wanted everything as it had always been, as it was before he'd gone.

All evening he and his father had ignored each other, purposefully stayed apart, each pretending not to know the other, not father and son. But later, Reggie had found himself standing trembling outside the door, unsure why. Standing quietly in the orchard now, looking out at the trees, he remembered how he'd stood there like a girl till Mary Beth came outside and found him. She took his hands and pulled him inside, got him to dance and made him forget. Turning her under his arm he'd looked up laughing and saw his father watching him. Reggie danced in place, unable to move or look away as Mary Beth turned. His father had nodded his head at him. Almost imperceptible. The moment of time between them across the dance floor. The nod was so slight Reggie could doubt it had even happened. His father nodding, keeping time with the music only. Reggie looked up as a bird flew over his head, wanting more, wanting his hand. That is what it had been Reggie decided. A trick of timing only. He pulled another crabapple pressed the pulp into his palm, opened his hand for the bird. He and his father had not gone up to each other after, had not spoken. Reggie had left with his cousins and Mary Beth, his father still playing. And nothing had changed. Everything still the same, unforgiven, unforgiving. The bird flew off as Reggie closed his hand. He shrugged his shoulders. He was useful here on the farm, wanted here. Unwanted there, and Reggie walked back across the orchard towards the field, his head down.

THE NEXT MORNING ALEX WALKED THE TOWN, trying to stay away from the river having dreamed the whole night through of water. He and Reggie were impossibly together swimming at the north shore, the wake of their bodies spreading into each other formed white crests of waves, like the rapids above the falls. The gleam and shimmer of the water, and the two of them together. Trying to forget, Alex walked up and down the streets, the town full of people, festive with its tables and umbrellas out on the hotel lawns, and everywhere anticipation. It was only midmorning when he returned to the river, unable to stop himself, wanting to see the man on the island, wanting to brand his eyes with it, the impossible made possible in front of him.

The riverbank was thronged with people and he had to push himself through to the front. He found Farini's brother next to a rope that was tied to a large tree up from the bank. And on the island, Farini was tying the other end of the rope to the largest tree there, windswept island caught in the falls, the few trees small and bent, keeping a tentative hold. He watched as Farini pressed against the rope, tried its tension. He saw how Farini pulled at it, tested its strength and the tree's. The rope was not far above the water, three feet maybe, as high as the tree on the island could hold. The line was angled up river so that it veered away from the edge of the falls. It was not the shortest distance over the open water, but away from the shifts in the currents of air above the falls, as far away as possible from the falls themselves. The crowd around Alex jostled and shoved, joked with each other. Alex was silent, knew what to watch for in a rope and he waited for Farini.

Farini seemed pleased with the rope and the knot he'd tied and walked back and forth stretching his shoulders. He rubbed his legs warming himself, loosening the stiffness from two nights of sleeping in the open. Still he didn't cross. Alex watched him, saw how Farini held one of his arms wrong. Hurt, hard to balance then. Farini's brother watched too, paced when Farini paced, stood when he stood. Waited.

Alex stepped back to the tree. The crowd in front of him watched the island; no one was watching him. He pulled on the rope testing its tautness as Farini had done. On the island Farini shook his head and sat down again. Alex took off his shoes and swung his legs up over the rope, like a child swinging on a bar, and pulled himself up to sitting and then to standing. Holding the trunk of the tree he looked out over the crowd to the island, and beyond the island, a new view of the falls. To his left were the vast Horseshoe Falls, and just beyond him the edge of the American Falls. The noise of both rose up at him as he stood five feet above the ground. He could feel the rope under his feet move with the vibrations from the sound and Alex trembled. He looked away from the falls and down at his feet. He breathed, calmed himself. He knew how to walk a rope. He walked forward a few steps and back again, bounced a little, tested the give. The rope felt good under his feet, familiar. The rope from the tree sloped down gently, just barely over the watchers' heads. Alex walked forward. He moved past the watchers as they looked up. No one stopped him. Farini's brother leaned forward to see Farini better, thinking the people were stirring because of his brother.

He did not see Alex until Alex stepped out beyond reach over the river.

Alex had never walked over water before, but Alex wasn't afraid of water. He could hear the play of the river, the splash of the small rapids against themselves. He walked almost half way to the island where the rope was lowest, just above the water. There the river's spray reached the rope and Alex felt the wet slip of the water under his feet. He moved forward another step, and another. Careful and slow. He was good at walking ropes. This was his first time over water, loving the feel of it, the sound of it. He stopped, closed his eyes, the wind a breeze of air cool on his head. He opened his eyes again, saw Farini stand and watch him. He walked forward two more steps and stopped. The two of them just stood, looked at each other, one over the river and the other on the edge of the island at the top of the falls.

Alex nodded at Farini, then turned around. He did not look at the crowd, but stared above their heads to the tree at the far end. Alex took a step back towards the shore and stopped, did not look back, did not look to see if Farini would step up onto the rope. Alex waited. The people on the shore waited, watched.

Farini turned away, walked to the other side of the island and looked at the falls. He rolled his shoulders and turned quickly. He walked back to the tree and pulled himself up onto the rope. Everyone was silent. There was only the sound of the water and the falls as Farini adjusted his balance. He placed his arms, careful with the one that was hurt. He took a breath, nodded to his brother.

Alex could feel Farini's weight on the rope. He sank closer to the river, ripples of cold water ran over the rope, over his feet beginning to turn numb. He felt Farini step forward. Alex relaxed himself, adjusted to the other's weight on the rope. He'd never walked a rope before with someone else, the two of them having to account for the other, leave space for the other to walk. The rope bent low over the water with the weight of two. They stepped almost in time, just slightly out of step so that neither was thrown off balance, the rope in a continual flux, a patterned shifting. Alex wanted to stop and listen to the falls again, be alone above the river. But Farini didn't stop, walked faster even than Alex could walk. Alex hurried, stepped less sure of himself; his foot slipped and he nearly fell. Farini, too, slipped on the opposite side, both of them off kilter. Farini stopped. Alex could hear the hum of a tune, quiet, soft like Ben on the rope, coaching him. The chant — look up, feel your feet, know the air. Alex took a breath. He took one step and paused. Farini waited. Alex walked forward again, a little faster, better than he was before, and sure of himself. He reached the riverbank. Really, it was not far; he'd walked farther on the brothers' line across the circus tent. Higher too. He'd only gone half way to the island, reached the mid-point of the river before he'd stopped and they'd looked at each other.

Alex did not step down at the river's edge. He didn't want to disrupt Farini who was out over the middle of the river now. Alex walked above the crowd and continued towards the tree and Farini continued towards the shore. Farini's brother was at the very edge of the river watching Farini and the watchers too, enthralled, watched Farini out over the river. When he reached the tree, Alex waited before he turned around. Farini reached the shore and fell into his brother's arms. The crowd kept back from the men, amazed now, that Farini was there beside them, a miracle, cheating death. Alex saw how the two men embraced, how they held each other, watched as their faces crumpled and how they turned away from the on-lookers. Alex was alone by the tree, the crowd lost in the brothers and the brothers lost in themselves, the rope stretching out over the water to the empty island. Alex felt as though he would break down, shake with sobs. He jumped down from the tree and grabbed his shoes, ran up the street before anyone turned to look for him. A minute later Farini and his brother craned their eyes through the crowd searching for the savior boy who couldn't be found.

Sunday, October 30th. Hotel Montreal

MERCY WROTE A LETTER HOME TO HER sister. She wished that Ide were there too, with her. Married now though, Married, though she was younger than Mercy. No need for her to come with them to Quebec. But it would have been fun together, Mercy thought. Ide would have seen the humour in it the same way Mercy did. She would have found the girls who monopolized the parlour, and the men, funny too.

The talks were over and they'd begun the tour. Montreal the first stop and she'd been well enough to attend the big banquet. Had danced the whole night and felt fine this morning. Well again! Danced with everyone. Danced with John A. And the rain had stopped, finally.

This morning they'd toured the city — gone up the mountain. A mountain on an island in the middle of a river, so unlike home. And she didn't want to think of home. There was nothing Mercy could say that would capture it all, or that Ide would understand. Ide was happy, happy with what she had. Mercy wanted more. She folded the letter into her journal, not wanting to talk of it, did not want to believe this would ever end.

Alex rushed up the side streets away from the centre of town, away from the falls and the river, away from the sound of the water, hurrying inland. He reached the edge of town and kept walking, the land becoming farmland, the road turning to gravel, loose stones rolling out from beneath his feet. It was not like home, clay hard roads, and his mind unable to tell what was different. He was crying now, didn't know why, the tears were running down his face. Just his stomach was in a whirl, unsettled. He passed a field of hay on his left and an orchard on his right, the smell of fruit fallen overripe unfamiliar too. The wind began to blow and Alex looked up. The clouds pulled into a skein, skin of a mackerel, skin sky of home. He walked till he tired himself out, till he couldn't walk any further, and he stopped by the edge of a field. Climbed over the ditch and leaned his back against a tree, closed his eyes and fell asleep.

Reggie left the orchard and walked back through the line of firs that edged the fields. It was darker beneath the trees and he didn't see his father until he was ten feet away from him. Reggie stopped. His father hadn't seen him. He was looking across the field, shading his eyes as he did on the boat, watching to see if something would appear. His father moved forward into the field, uncomfortable under the trees, liking the open. Reggie watched him. What was he here for? Reggie shrugged his shoulders, put his hands in his pockets. If he stayed by the trees he could pass by unnoticed, leave his father be. Reggie almost felt he had intruded where his father didn't expect him. He walked a few more steps closer under the trees and a crow above him cawed. His father turned around, saw him. The two of them looked at each other, both silent. Till Reggie, unable to stand there any longer with neither of them saying anything, blurted, "I'm not coming back, if that's what you're after."

"No," his father paused, was silent again.

Always a surprise on Sundays, his father looking like neither a fisherman nor a farmer, dapper in his suit and hat. It unsettled Reggie. His father said nothing more and the two of them just looked at each other, the only sound that of the crow as it cawed again. Reggie looked at the trees to the side, away from his father, shrugged again. Waiting so long he had to look back to make sure his father was there.

"You're better off seasick than dead, Reggie." His father was at the edge of the field bright in the sun, Reggie under the trees in the cool of the shade smelling the resin of the windbreak of pines. The smell of land, the smell of trees, his father never having said anything ever about his being sick, as if he didn't notice, as if it never happened.

He looked at his father. "Why'd you make me go?" He shook his head, his voice soft. "Why every day?"

"They're calling in the troops from Halifax, Reggie. There'll not be just stand-offs and songs anymore." His father stood with his arms by his side not looking directly at Reggie.

"You had Alex." Reggie looked down, turned away. "Alex loved it."

Louder, "They'll be using guns against your straw men, against your pipes pretending to be guns." Fletcher's field, the story renown, scarecrows and haystacks with pipes that had

fooled the collectors who'd turned tide at the sight. His father
waved his arm, the straw men and pipes knocked away.

"Why did you need me?" Softer yet, "Why couldn't you let
me . . . " Reggie stopped. He did not look up at his father.
"There was Alex." His shoulders slumped, the air gone from
him.

"Are you not listening, Reggie. I'm here to . . . "

"What are you here for then, father?" Reggie turned fast
and looked at him. "To save me, protect me? I'm better here.
Do you want to happen to me what happened to Alex? Dead,
drowned, father." His voice broke. "Where else, what else?"
He looked at his father who seemed small in his suit, his hat
shading his eyes. Wiry and slight like Alex, both fishermen,
not like Reggie, broad-backed, thick limbed, meant for weight,
anchor of bone, meant to sink. Reggie looked away.

His father turned and looked out to the field. He bowed
his head, then looked at Reggie. He took something from his
pocket. "Your mother is sending you this." He held out his
hand.

Reggie looked at him, did not move forward, his face
broken not wanting to cry. No word then, no news of Alex. His
father's arms lifted slightly from his side. He walked towards
Reggie. "Here."

Reggie paused, took his hand from his pocket. His father
looked a moment at Reggie's palm stained red, thinking it was
blood. Looked as if he would lay his finger, trace the cut line
of his son's palm, then stopped himself. He lay a pocket watch
in Reggie's hand.

"You're needed at home Reggie," his father said and walked
past him up through the trees to the road. "Don't forget. You're
still my son."

He drove away as Reggie looked at the watch. Alex's watch. And no Alex. Brought to him, for him to keep, for him to look after. As he hadn't looked after Alex. Token of guilt, token of loss. His now. He knew that. Forever. He opened it.

Someone had wound it. The watch ticked at him, the ship on its dial going nowhere. Where Alex had gone. While Reggie was here, safe in the field. His father's wagon was gone from view now. Reggie was alone, Alex's watch in his hand, the ship against the blue of the sky riding the road ahead of him, leaving him.

THERE WERE SWALLOWS IN THE TREE OVERHEAD and the long light shadows of fall stretched across the field towards Alex and woke him. He was unsure where he was for a moment, had forgotten his walk over the river, Farini, the island on the edge of the falls. And then he heard the wind through the trees, a few leaves fluttering like the song of water beginning. Alex stood. He climbed over the ditch, the grass rustling too, the noise singing in his ears. He turned back the way he'd come, walked down the road, retracing his steps. Placing his feet where he thought he saw the marks of his shoes, a childish game. Turning and walking backwards, his feet facing forward like he had done when he was a child, a game to fool the others, disappearing with his feet. Like his walk at the falls, the steps forwards then backwards, turning on the rope and walking back, he'd nodded not so much at Farini as at himself. Because he'd wanted to keep going. He wanted the rope to stretch further, cross the island, reach out toward the falls, over the falls. He would have kept going, walked the air over the water. If Farini had not been there, if he had not caught Alex's eye and made Alex look at him, acknowledge him, Alex would have kept on, crossed the island on foot and stepped out into the water.

Even here the wind through the trees was singing the song of water, calling him, pulling him to it. Alex longed for water, the feel of it, the touch of it through him and he walked faster back towards the town, back towards the falls.

Monday, October 31st. Parliament Buildings, Ottawa

JOHN A STEPPED OUT, LEADING THEM ALL in a Pied Piper walk down to the locks, too tight to finish his speech, needing air. He knew they wanted to stay warm and dry up in the Picture Gallery in the new parliament buildings drinking their port or their coffee. But he wanted, needed to be outside and he led them away down the steep hill to the locks. Some slipped, the sky threatened rain, and the clouds above the river were as gray as the river itself. The wind blew and the air smelled of the river and the earth, the leaves that had fallen. Shafts of sun broke through the cloud, fell on the group of them and the air was sweet with leftover summer and the rain of fall before the winter, before it all died and became new again. The way it always was.

They followed Macdonald, whether they wanted to or not, to see the locks emptying and filling. To watch the boats travel in and out, into the canal, through the locks into the Great Lakes, all the way in to Superior or out. John A stopped, watched a boat being lowered into the Ottawa River. The whole country connected by water. East to the St. Lawrence, to the sea. And west, Rupert's Land, the Northwest Territories. And the Pacific. Ripe. His. All would join, come. He could see it. Eventually. Even Prince Edward Island, without the money the Canadians had promised, without promises at all. They would join. After all, George Coles had stood in John A's stead at lunch, praised the union, when John A himself couldn't continue. All he had to do was talk and talk and talk, bend the men, sway the people. The men and the country would fall together. He was pulling the country as it danced together. A song started in John A's head as he watched the boats and he sang aloud as the others turned away, eager to leave.

Mercy and her father walked together following in Macdonald's steps. The river below them was visible but not the locks, their view blocked by the hill covered with trees, by the sumacs turned red. The path was wet with rain, more rain. The water here inland, away from the sea, was endless, she thought, and her heel slipped and she nearly fell. She reached forward just in time to catch her father's arm and stopped herself from falling.

She liked the smell of rain, of fall, a day that brought winter that would bring spring, and summer again. Summer so close to fall she could forget how long it would be till summer came again. In fall summer seemed just around the corner and now it was as if they were truly in summer, the height of things yet to come. Mercy and her father reached an open spot on the path where the hill levelled for a moment and they stopped to look out over the locks. She could hear John A, his words lilting out in the open air, the story of the river and of the locks, man-made wonders, augmenting God's plans.

"Ah, Mercy girl, what a day!" Her father, loving the wind, waved his arms at the clouds and the river as if it were sea.

Like a fall day of home when he walked along the harbour, an afternoon haunt, walking the edge of the pier always a thrill.

They were the last pair down to the locks. Mercy looked at the bank on the other side of the canal, saw a steep red gold hill covered in trees that seemed to slip down its side.

"Like home," he said.

Mercy smiled. Loving him, still, always, more now in this world of away. With possibilities, possibilities that she wanted, hadn't expected. Of away, of leaving. Of more. She took his hand. River, canals, locks, steep hills of red trees — nothing like home.

"Look." She reached out and almost touched a dragonfly, its wings frosted like sugared candy and its body as red as the leaf it sat on. "Are you headed home or away?" she asked it. "Late in the year to be leaving now. You're better off home," she said, not even thinking. They turned away as they heard John A's voice again and looked down to the locks. The others were far ahead, wanted away, and John A was talking to himself. Mercy realized he was singing. A fragment of a sea shanty drifted up to them and her father laughed and sang the next line so only he and Mercy could hear. Mercy let go of his arm and danced two steps of a jig and her father danced beside her. John A watching out at the locks did not see Mercy and her father, and he tapped the ground, kept time with his foot as father and daughter and country followed the would-be lover down to the river halfway between home and away.

ALEX WALKED QUICKLY DOWN THE ROAD. IT was after five o'clock already, the circus's afternoon show Alex had forgotten was over. The arms that would have caught him, Ben, Henry,

Will, forgot Alex too. He had gone as he had come, their arms empty with air.

Alex reached the edge of town and hurried up the street following the sound of water. He wanted to see the rope over the river again. When he arrived, no one was there. Trembling, he reached his hand out and felt for the rope, made sure it was still tied. It was. Alex took off his shoes. Climbed up onto the rope. Stood. He did not look out at the river, nor at the island, or at the falls. The rope in the early evening light was almost invisible and Alex watched straight ahead at the mist over the water. He was alone like he wanted to be, alone at the water that reached to the falls. He stepped forward. Pulled by the feel of the rope beneath him, by the sound of water, Alex walked past the edge of the riverbank, over the easy ripples of water along the shore, walked past where he'd turned back earlier.

He was beyond the middle of the river, farther than he'd walked earlier. Alex stopped, paused, knew he shouldn't look down and did anyway. He looked at the rope beneath his feet and at the water below him. The water rose in dark swells. He'd expected the small white waves like those he saw from the shore. The rope swayed. He closed his eyes, waited. He looked up away from the rope, away from the water. His eyes were dry. He shut his eyes, opened them and closed them again. There was a barrage of sound around him, the noise of the two falls was deafening, tangible in the air. The rope quivered with the roar, made Alex tremble. Never in Alex's experience had sound held a rope. He felt now if the sound were to stop, the rope would fall, and he too. All of them, rope, water and Alex, tempted by the siren sound of the fall of water. Alex was pulled forward, like the water, tempted, just another step and another. Come closer, closer, it sang. And he walked on, couldn't help himself. Alex kept moving on out over the water. Until he was stopped by the tree at the end of the line without ever seeing he'd gotten there. He touched his hand to his face. Both hand and face wet with mist as he leaned into the trunk of the tree, and there, just beyond him, he saw the very edge of the water falling away.

FOUR

Then let us be firm and united —
One country, one flag for us all;
United our strength will be freedom —
Divided we each of us fall.

— Programme of Toasts, Montreal,
Thursday October 27th, 1864

Farini

ONCE, ALMOST TWO YEARS BEFORE, AT THE Italian Opera in Havana on the island of Cuba, Farini's wife, riding on his back, gave a merry wave. Impromptu, off cue. Out of sync and off time as Farini continued moving forward and she was left behind, held back in her wave. And she began to fall behind him, tipping backwards off his back. Until Farini let go of his pole, let himself fall too, his arm reaching out behind him. Falling till he hung from his knees, reached out and caught her as she fell past: the shimmer of her dress, its beautiful material translucent in the light held in his hand, ripping, the pull of the earth, the material ripping and his hand held nothing but a piece of cloth.

Just once.

REGGIE, ALEX, AND HIS FATHER WERE OUT in the boat as Reggie looked up. There, marching toward them, were the soldiers who had come from Halifax, marching right over them, swamping the boat. The boat began to sink and Reggie and his father clung to the sides as everything slipped past, the fish and lines and nets floating above them as they sank with the boat. Alex was there too. He swam in circles over their heads, but Reggie was too afraid to reach for Alex's hand, too afraid to let go of the boat. He and his father sank and Reggie shuddered; he was suffocating, needed to breathe. Reggie's mouth opened and it filled with water. He cried out, waking himself. He was only half awake and thought he was home, that it was time to get up, time to go fishing. Panic welled up in him, left the taste of salt tears on his lip.

Reggie sat up quickly. Never. Never again out on the water. He looked out the window, wanted the bed to stop its sea sway, his stomach sick, tears in his eyes each time it happened. Never escaping the sea, everywhere his stomach sick. He hated it.

He was unable to fall back to sleep and lay listening to the rain that started suddenly and heavily. The whole weight of rain and wet on Reggie who turned to the wall. No one thinks they'll find him alive, his uncle had said to the neighbour yesterday afternoon. Reggie listening silently, had been furious. Lucky to find him at all, the neighbour had responded. Reggie had felt suddenly sick then and had to leave the room in a rush. Now his father had brought him Alex's watch. It was Reggie's now. The responsibility was his. One son was gone — but it was the second born. And Reggie was the first. It is the first born who never leaves. But Reggie had left, had broken all the rules. He was supposed to be the one to stay. Talisman of safety, the first to be born, the first to . . . He left the thought unfinished. And his father, that too. That too, he'd left. God damn them.

Reggie pulled off the covers and got out of bed. He dressed and left the house. The birds were out now calling and the rain had stopped, the sun shimmered on the fields making them look like water. The long grass rippled in the wind as though

ANNE McDONALD

in a wave. The whole sky was reflected in a puddle ahead of
him. Water. On the land that he loved water, staring back at
him everywhere water. Listening, he heard the sigh of wind
through the trees and the grass, like the wind on the boat
when they turned out to the open sea. A rare wind blowing
north pushed at his back. He watched as the grass in the field
rolled like waves through the sea. Rolling forward, pushed
like him, away, and Reggie walked up the road away from the
house, away from the farm. Walked without stopping, more
than an hour, straight through the field that turned into sand
that slipped out from beneath his feet, the grass of the dunes
waving like the field, the wind pushing stronger at his back, all
the way to the edge of the sea.

Tuesday, November 1st. Train to Cobourg

THEY LEFT OTTAWA IN THE MORNING AND travelled by train
away from the river. From the window Mercy saw forests of
trees almost bare of leaves, white trunks of birch upon birch, a
few lemon leaves left to wave at them as they went by. So many
trees and so much land, silver patches of water in the sun,
lakes that were impossibly small. Until they finally reached
Kingston and the lake looked so large Mercy thought it had
to be sea.

They stopped in Kingston and she watched as John A
stepped from the train and onto the platform. The crowd
became loud with noise when they saw him. His hometown,
his people, Mercy was amazed by the numbers, by how they
called for Macdonald. It was so loud she could hardly hear

what he said. Her father and all the Maritimers were brought forward to meet the crowd, John A praising them and her father beside him bowed and waved at the cheering people.

John A smiled as he moved out onto the platform with a surety of step. His chest expanded. How he loved a crowd. He was nothing without them. When he was alone the quiet of home sometimes descended like a din. The band played and the crowd cheered more, and when the men stepped back into the carriage they slapped one another on the back and congratulated each other and John A smiled more.

They stopped in towns all along the shore of the lake and there were more speeches and bands. Fanfare, a party everywhere and everywhere they were late, the sun beginning to set and the sky turning pink and red in a twilight of blue, bluer than anything Mercy had seen at home while the land seemed to stretch and stretch and stretch ahead of them. The stars were out by the time they finally reached Cobourg for dinner and Mercy was starving. Late there too, the Solicitor General showed them in to dinner and got them ready to leave all at the same time with less than an hour to eat. It was a mad rush and everyone was caught up in the frenzy, speaking quickly, loudly, barely sitting down to dinner before getting back up again.

And then the most wonderful thing. Before they could leave, they were ushered out to the back lawn. They stood on the grass that had dewed over, Mercy's shoes and ankles wet with it, to watch a display of fireworks. All of them with their heads back, waited, watched silent with anticipation like children poised for wonder and awe. And then the sound, which Mercy loved the best, as it echoed off the stone of the building into the ground and into her. She tasted the smoke in the air, watched it drift across the sky. So caught up that she did not at first hear Macdonald's voice beside her.

"What worlds we create when we want." Returning his flask. Clouds blew in across the lake, making it warm, dark. He paused. "As though the stars and moon weren't enough for us, we create something more." Endless possibilities. He breathed deeply.

He was standing close beside Mercy. She did not look at him, replied, "But neither the moon or stars make noise."

Macdonald nodded, "A nightly fanfare of their arrival is what they need. Yes, both a prospect and a voice ," he continued.

Mercy could tell he'd turned to look at her and had looked away again. She turned slightly towards him, smiled to herself. "The voice affects the view, don't you think?"

"A good thing in my case." The ugliest man in Canada, his sister's loving teasing.

"Well, that might be said, Mr. Macdonald," but she laughed at the same time. The night was warm, a light wind blew on her face, the smell of water - lake and rain, in the air. "It's a beautiful night," she said and turned towards him.

John A looked around him, "Though the darkness obscures the beauty and blocks my view."

"I thought you said if something were not before your eyes, you forgot it, Mr. Macdonald."

He laughed. "You don't forget anything, don't let it slip and slide away from you, do you?"

"And you? Do you remember only what you want to remember?" The two still watched up at the sky.

"Shorter that way. An abbreviated and abridged history. Easier."

She smiled. "But untrustworthy, untrue."

"And true is only what you can see." The last of the fireworks an echo of sound in the air and the smoke a lazy breeze headed back towards home.

"You're not playing fair. Putting words in my mouth and leading me astray . . . playing games with me." The others around them hurried again, this a lull in the storm of excited anticipation, ready to move on. Ottawa to Toronto in a day and all the stops along the way, building towards the real event, Toronto. Mercy and John A with their heads turned up yet towards the sky, the moon only a halo of light through cloud and smoke.

"No, I'm a man who likes to say what he means." He paused, looked at her. "And I always mean it when I say it." A pretend serious nod.

She turned and looked at him. "Transient then, like the fireworks. Not steady like the stars." They were the last pair on the lawn, the others were moving back through the house.

He pointed above her head. The sky cleared, his arm grazed hers. "The stars shift and move depending upon where you are and what time it is. That star right there may have already extinguished its flame. And yet we see it." He lowered his arm, looked at her. "So is it true or not true?"

"We are deceived then. Or worse, we deceive ourselves, knowingly believing in something that might not be real." Mercy paused, shrugged her shoulders. "Fools then." She could feel the sigh of his breath on her neck.

"I can't live that way." His voice was serious now, not joking. He looked at her, was on the verge of falling in love. "I believe while I see it, albeit knowing that the world changes while I live in it."

They stood in the dark, even the sound of the others gone now, the house empty. Mercy turned to walk along the path by the side of the house, wanting to stay out in the cool of the evening, the smell of rain in the air, not wanting to leave, lingering. She turned back to Macdonald. "And what about a falling star? How do you explain that to yourself when you see one?"

John A smiled. She was as good as he was, this play, this talk. "Oh, I never look. I look away, of course, not wanting to see my world end before my eyes." He followed her on the path as she knew he would.

Mercy laughed. "You're a con artist, fooling everyone." She walked with her head turned up at the sky. And he reached out his hand to her arm, stopping her.

"Not now, I don't deceive you this time." He pointed to the ground, about to step into a puddle of water. "The wet of your feet would prove me true."

They were stopped on the path, his hand on her arm. "And otherwise?" she asked, looked directly at him.

Yes, feeling the night swell of air in the trees. Almost hearing the sound of a wave on the shore of the lake, yes. "As true as the moon or the sun, even though they turn away from us." The two having to step close together past the water. "You believe in the moon, don't you?"

They came to the front of the house, the carriages already leaving and he helped her into the carriage with her mother and Mrs. Alexander and to her surprise, stepped in himself. He entertained them all the way, told them what they would see on their way to Niagara Falls, after Toronto. The land past Toronto, on the other side of the lake pastoral, orchards of fruit trees, fertile, soft and gentle all the way to the falls. The sound and the mist of them giving warning, though not fair enough, not expecting to find the land fallen away. The water in a flow, unable to stop itself. He turned his head to look out the window. Ah, John, he said to himself. You're waxing poetic. Love and all before you, so easy now, fall in love, lie in bed, a drink, just one, a few more speeches. Yes now. He was ready, the speech he'd give tonight. Toronto waiting, and the tour. Yes the falls. The sound of his voice like a song in his head, a rhythm of noise pulling him forward, unable to stop too.

Mercy looked through the window, saw only her reflection in the dark. Yes, the moon. She did believe in the moon. An islander after all, of the sea. And the moon's pull, the tide of her rising, pulled ever closer.

John A talked on, "You'll see. We'll go to Table Rock, a window under the falls, and you'll see. The falls are a screen of water before you as you stand under and behind the very falls themselves. Unbelievable, that the earth has created those tunnels, that we can stand there and the rock does not crumble away." John A leaned forward, "It is unbelievable and yet one is wet with the falls as it sprays in at us. It is almost too much to imagine. Or too much to believe? Even though it is there in front of our eyes." He paused, leaned back, his hands raised from his lap, "And yet real." He shrugged, looked back at them. "Odd how that is. Some things so insignificant, so trifling it hardly matters whether you believe or not. And others so significant that you can't possibly believe them. Like death. Like love, though they are so. The nature of belief." He paused, smiled at Mercy, "But you know that better than me . . . the one with faith."

ALL NIGHT, LYING ON THE ISLAND IN Farini's bed of grass, Alex heard the water running past, heard the waves as they licked at the shore, the sucking sound of water against land. These were the sounds he heard above the noise of the falls. All day he'd watched the water from every angle of the island. At the head the water splashed up, spraying him as it divided itself, separated round the island. He'd placed fallen twigs into the water and then walked the shore quickly, following their path. Some sticks were submerged, sinking before they even rounded the island and others rode the waves and were caught in the currents that eddied past. He always stopped watching as they moved past the island, headed over the falls. Alex not quite ready yet for the more that would be.

People were gathering on the riverbank, watching him and Alex sat on the far side of the island, away from the watchers. This wasn't for them, a spectacle or a show. He wanted to see, wanted to know the island at the edge of the falls. Almost the more he'd always wanted. A bird landed on the rock close by him and then stepped into the water. It floated there in the calm of the lee of the island and Alex watched it swim, keeping its place as it faced upstream away from the falls. The bird watched him too. He was an unusual sight on her island, this place for birds. Alex watched the bird slowly float past him, watched beyond where he'd given up on the sticks, saw it taken toward the edge. A sense of panic as the bird did nothing, did not fly away, just floated watching him on the island, ignoring the falls. Alex stood quickly as the bird disappeared beyond his sight, the bird gone over the edge. Only a moment in time before it rose and flew away. Leaving Alex feeling panicked and foolish. Silly as a spectator, his lack of faith.

He sat back down, stared out, looked where he hadn't looked before, at the water disappearing over the edge. He moved to the end of the island, the water at his feet. A puddle was caught in a crevice of the island and Alex reached out his foot to it. Warm rock water, Alex sat there with his foot held in the water till the sun began to sink. He inched closer to the end of the island where the rapids sprayed up and put his foot in the water there, his body recoiling with the shock of the cold. But he did not move. He stayed seated, his ankle going numb, no more than the length of his body away from the edge of the falls.

Finally Alex pulled his foot out and lay down. He fell asleep at the end of the island, dreaming that Reggie was sleeping beside him. He slept all night through as if he were home, he and Reggie and their father rising early and going off to the boat before anyone else would be up. This the sound around him now, surrounded by water like on their boat. On his boat island dreaming everything wrong. No one was out on the boat, his father was alone and Reggie was gone. But Alex knew none of that, dreaming home as though it were the same. Sleeping hungry he thought he was eating bread and molasses, warm bun filling his mouth, seeming so real. He woke because he bit down hard on his tongue. The wind was blowing white clouds past the moon shining full, sliding west over the falls, and the stars blinded, fell faint against the sky. Alex turned towards the water, watched the moon, salt blood, like sea, like home on his lip.

ENDLESS AIR OF SALT AND WATER, SALT on his face and in his mouth, all the world water and sky as Reggie sat at the edge of the sea. He stayed there all day watching the water as though he were waiting for Alex. He hated his uncle, hated his neighbour, and his father, all who believed Alex dead. Unwilling, unable to believe what he'd said himself. He waited all the day till the sun began to set and Reggie lowered his head onto his arms. The tide came in, rolled up over his feet and still he sat. He raised his head, watched as the sun turned red and the sky gold, then pink. Alex was gone and Reggie was sick knowing what he hadn't understood before. There would be no reunion. He and Skip would not rush down the road to meet Alex. Only Skip was left to love Alex as though he hadn't died, loving him as though he'd never left. Only those believing Alex hadn't died able to love him like before, hope loving hope. Some of Reggie died with this change of heart, change of thought. If Alex were to show up now, return unharmed, it would be different. Those who had given up hope had grieved already. If Alex were to suddenly return, they'd be untrusting, wary that Alex would disappear again, just as he'd appeared, all their grief and worry fruitless in the end. Reggie becoming wary now too, unwilling, unable to trust.

But Reggie hadn't cried. He wished that he would, that he could, cry. Could break this dry spell of watching, of waiting for Alex. Alex, who no one thought would ever be seen again.

It was night when he finally stood and looked out at the sea. Black sea and black sky, the white crests of waves the only things visible. There was nothing and no one else there and Reggie turned abruptly and walked away. He walked up to the dunes, found where one curved into the other giving protection from the wind and he lay down in the sand. He held himself close against the sea damp air, against the sea itself that wouldn't leave him be, sick on land and water. His father always wanting more, Alex gone, and now his father needing Reggie more than ever.

It was never what Reggie wanted. He rolled over, lay on his side. He'd have to go back. He shivered, closed his eyes. The sea would take him too, eventually, that's how it would be. He was neither, not a fisherman nor a farmer, the unfirst son, nothing and alone. He fell asleep as the moon rose full, shone almost as bright as day and the wind shifted. Mackerel sky of day, a storm in the night, the noise of the waves pounding on the shore played in Reggie's head, curled into himself against the cold, against the sound.

Tuesday, November 1st, evening. Queens Hotel, Toronto

MACDONALD WAS THE LAST TO GET OUT of the carriage, his tongue thick, thirsty. He wanted a drink. The streets were full of people already, their torchlights flickering in the rain and he rode in the carriage to the stables at the back of the hotel. He wanted to go in by himself, wanted to stop for a drink. He knew the other men would be upstairs already, preparing to speak. There had been masses of people and the carriage was slow trying to move through them. He drained his flask and finally stepped out into the rain. The night changed from stars and smoke to wet and mud. Macdonald went into the tavern and ordered a bottle of gin for his room. He'd go up with the men soon. From the bar he could hear the crowds outside, anxious for the speeches, anxious for the union, for the bigness, the grandeur of a country. His chest swelled. It was happening. He would speak tonight and in all the towns of Canada West and East, talking and talking. Because he could do it, he could make them see, make them want it. He could make it happen, this country.

Upstairs in his room he took off his coat and drank as he stood by the fire. He could hear the men in the room down the hall as he took out his pipe, just one pipe and then he'd go over. He poured himself another drink. Yes, that's how it would be. He settled in his chair, closed his eyes for a moment. He was a practical man. Here was the country, ready, waiting. He sighed. He was a practical man wanting to fall, wanting to stop, and fall in love — in the midst of work, wanting to leave it all for the others. He would live out his days happily at the edge of her island watching the shore drift in and out — not even fooling himself. Just now, just as it always was, when he'd worked so long and hard, now he would, wanted to, wished he could fall in love, and forget, forget it all. Even for a few months, if he could stop, lose himself.

John A stood. He knew how it was. He knew what would happen. He would work till he broke, and then he'd drink. He'd drink so much that he wouldn't remember, wake somewhere new, maybe head south again. A binge alone, or a new friend. Not knowing where he was or how he'd gotten there. And not caring. That was the blessed, lovely thing about it — the not caring. He drank again. Not yet though, not yet. He walked over to the bed. This time, this time it could work. He looked at the fire, the flames bright, red, like the sun, the island soil. It was perfect, falling in love amidst speeches and balls, dancing, the island a charm. He could fall in love, continue.

He lay down, stretched out, his drink in his hand. He raised himself on his elbow, drank. He made half an attempt to get up. He could go over, stand with them. He didn't need to speak tonight. He could celebrate with them. There were plenty of others to speak tonight. He raised his head, drank again. The men began their speeches out on the balcony and John A was unable to hear them, the quiet, the peace, his eyes closing thinking of swimming. Why hadn't he swum? He'd go back, he and his son, next summer just like this summer in that low island wind, the slow caress of his own hand on his forehead and drank again. Yes, that's what they'd do. He forgot his speech, and he and Mercy could dance the very next dance. Sighing, thinking of Mercy as Isabel — so much easier to just think of Isa, darling and dead. His eyes closed as he fell asleep, gin drunk and alone.

Mercy could not sit still. In the parlour of the hotel the women were drinking tea, waiting for the men to finish their speeches upstairs. She stood and went to the table, poured herself more tea and then left her cup and went over to the bookshelf. She ran her hand along the spines and pulled out a book of poetry. She opened it and read the first few lines, twice reading them and still could not remember what she'd read. She placed the book back on the shelf. She walked to the door and then to the window. Heavy curtains blocked the light and sound. When they'd arrived they had to make their way through the people gathered on the street in front of the hotel. All up and down the street people and more people were arriving — a torchlight parade. Even in the spits of rain and ten o'clock at night and there were people everywhere. She'd wanted to stand outside with them. She'd hoped John A would suggest it, take her arm as they exited the carriage and walk through the street out in the night with everyone else. That's what she'd wanted. But he stayed in the carriage as it drove back towards the stables and she and her mother and Mrs. Alexander were escorted inside by the hotel people.

The clock on the fireplace ticked. The pins in her hair stuck into her head. She sat down. Her chair sagged in the middle forcing her to sit back, her feet not touching the floor. Mercy stood up and her mother looked at her. Maybe you're overtired, her mother said. Maybe you ought to try going to bed and Mercy thought, yes. To leave would be better. She'd open her window and look out at the street, see the torches flicker below her, hear the people. Be above the men as they gave their speeches, listen to John A. She leaned down and kissed her mother good night and went up the stairs, passed the room with the men, heard their laughter and voices through the closed door.

In her room she sat on the bed. It was hot with the fire, the room too small and the night warm with the rain. She took off her hat, unpinned her hair and lay back on the bed. The noise of the crowd outside was barely audible through the windows and curtains. She sat again and stared at the fire. She stood and walked to the window, pulled back the edge of curtain, the light from the room below her spilling out onto the balcony and into the street. They must be nearly ready. The people below were hidden under their torches, a dance of light drizzled by rain if she blurred her eyes. She let the curtain go and it fell back over the window. The sound dull, muted. She walked to the fireplace and did not look into the mirror over it. She touched her fingers to her face, her cheeks hot. She ran her fingers over the smooth marble of the mantlepiece, then along the polished wood of the table. Ran her fingers over all the smooth and polished surfaces of the room.

In a sudden movement she turned to the door and went out, without hat or coat, her hair unpinned and falling loose. She went down the back stairs so she wouldn't be seen, to the door at the side of the hotel next to the stables. She gasped when she opened the door and saw the crowd of people so close, so loud there in the street. Mercy hesitated, thought about going back inside then shrugged her shoulders, smiled. She was absorbed into the flow as the crowd turned towards the avenue that went down to the lake. A parade up and down the street as the crowed chanted and cheered, calling for the men. They turned as they got to the avenue and Mercy, on the far side, looked south and there was the lake, there the moon, freeing itself of clouds, full. The highest tides now, even this fresh water lake shifting at full moon. There was excitement and anticipation in the air that was warm with everyone so close, their arms touching each other and Mercy didn't even notice the rain. The whole crowd turned back towards the middle of the street, pulled too, a tide rising, waiting to hear the men, the country ripe for a change, like Mercy.

She stood below the balcony and raised her head with the others and called out. The crowd erupted in cheers as the men stepped onto the balcony. Brown was in front. It was his town, his hour and he waved his hand at them and no one heard anything he said. Mercy like the others so eager, waiting and wanting — so caught in the moment, in the clamor, so caught up in themselves that it didn't matter anymore what was said. The men smiled foolishly as they tried to speak, their exhaled words visible drifted down into the upturned faces, into Mercy's mouth. Cheering and stamping her feet, clapping her hands, calling till her voice was hoarse. Mercy with all the others was wet with rain and mist in her hair and on her face, rain drops on her eyelashes and on her lips. She raised her hand to her face, no gloves either, brushed her fingers over her eyes and her cheeks, pushed the hair out of her face, the touch of wet skin on skin.

IN THE MORNING ALEX WOKE STIFF AND cold on Farini's island, his body cramped, held tight while he slept, the ground beneath him hard. He watched as the sun rose over the land, the water so dark it could be land and he lay curled into himself keeping warm as the light reached the falls and then the island. He opened his hands, stretched out his legs and watched the edge of the falls, the water a paler green right there. The light created an oddness of view, an altered perception, the water looking as though it played on the edge, never fell away. It was an optical illusion in the early morning. The crest of green right at the edge looked as if it were the sea off their boat. That was when Alex longed to swim, when he couldn't, the fishing lines trailing in their wake as they turned for home or out. He wanted to swim now, to feel the water, how it held him. It had been so long. He watched the play of the water, knew he could do it. Wanting the water at the edge of the falls, that green wake. Alex stood, walked over to the tree and untied the rope.

MERCY RETURNED TO HER ROOM IN THE dark, the night drizzled with stars and spits of rain, her hair soaked through when she touched it. She sat down by the fire and brushed her hair. It has been a trip of water, everything and everywhere wet. Away from water and into water. John A was right, an islander could never escape, bringing water with her wherever she went. Her clothes were wet too as she undressed slowly. She got into bed thinking of him when he'd walked beside her, so close she could feel him and yet not touching. The pull of him to her and her to him. Nothing physical that could break something so intangible as air. She lay back, her hair falling wet against her face and wet on the back of her neck. She reached up and pushed it back, thinking, God it will be a mess in the morning, curling with the rain and the damp. Loose strands of it escaping from pins and hats. She lay back with her eyes open.

Mercy closed her eyes, waited, then rose. She put a blanket over her shoulders and went to the window again, pulled back the curtain. No one was outside now, the light from the balcony below her was out. Everyone away to sleep, the night done. Not tired, Mercy went to the door and out into the hall, walked past John A's door to her parents' room and tapped softly. There was no answer, they were asleep too and she went back to her room. She paused in the hall outside, waited for a moment and turned her head to look behind her just in case, before she stepped back inside, and closed the door. She got back into bed and under the covers thinking the whole night through of the Canadas, land of falls and trees, huge lakes and rivers that didn't end. Lying with her arms outstretched, she was the land they travelled over, more and more and more of her. A never ending spreading open to the sky and the wind, the touch of air over her body. Never having to stop, always more. All the night through, falling in love alone.

IN THE MORNING REGGIE LAY CRADLED IN the sand that had shifted beneath him. He took his finger and ran a line across it, watched the small grains roll away till they fell together again out of his reach. He turned onto his back and stretched out his legs. The sun was rising; it found a break between the dunes sheltering him and shone into his eyes. He could hear the water behind him. The wind had blown all night and now the waves were landing heavily and he heard the sound of their crashing and the sucking of them as they pulled back down the shore. He licked his lip, his mouth was dry, tasted only of salt. He raised his hand and brushed it against his face; sand fell into his mouth. He rose and brushed his clothes. A fine coating of sand remained, lines on the crease of his arm where it had been curled under his head, the markings of where he'd been held. A shore of land, a shore of sea, both, neither one without the other. Reggie turned, walked back towards the water.

The wind had begun to die down and only the waves close to shore broke white. He walked along the edge of the sea where the sand rose in a dried ridge that crumbled beneath his feet. He was walking the border between sea and land, keeping his eyes down. Looking neither left or right he walked past pools of water left behind by the tide. He tried to keep his eyes away from any bit of water. It was a game he was playing, walking the narrow line of dry shore.

Trying to keep his eyes averted, he nearly stepped into a puddle. He stopped. A fish lay there, a faint bubble of air came from its mouth, its tail moving as his toe nudged the water. Trapped by the tide, held in the sand, and the water seeping away. Reggie stepped past it, the ugliness of it so close. How had it ever gotten there? Blown in by the wind and pulled by the tide. It had lost its way, a fish gone astray. He stepped past it not wanting to see, kept his eyes down, and walked away.

Wednesday, November 2nd. Toronto

In the morning Mercy rose, untired. They toured the city, the delegates and the women shown the sights. The first stop was the Lawyers Hall where the centre room reached all the way to the roof and they stood and looked up at a dome made completely of stained glass. The light from the dome was filtered and shimmered along the walls and the floor of mosaic. It made Mercy feel dizzy with her head back, staring up. Her hair fell over her forehead and into her face and across her eyes as she knew it would. Her sleepless night and waiting, the air so still in the room and she was breathless. The room a fall of water, the coloured light playing over their skin. Anticipation the whole night through, wanting to see him.

But he wasn't there.

Alex made a sailor's knot at the end of the rope that had been tied to the tree. A knot to hold a boat to its pier, one that wouldn't loosen as it was pulled. He stepped inside the loop and pulled the rope up under his arms. The water moved in small white waves, innocent, deceptive ripples along the surface close to the island. The sun was warm on Alex, leftover summer in fall. Alex stepped into the water. Sudden and cold, the shock made the skin under his arms tingle, just like home: a late summer swim, loving it. He swam and was held in place by his rope. He dove under, heard the sound of the falls like the wind in a storm caught on the boat, the wind water roar making the waves rise, crest white. He pushed himself to the surface and looked at the water further out where the river moved fast in green lines towards the falls. Alex wanted it, wanted the pull, wanted the edge, his rope tight around him.

He moved forward just a little more, away from the curved lee of the island, the breakwater behind him, and was caught in the current all in a moment and pulled under. Pushed and pulled. Alex loved the crazy spin of it, the wild pull like the days of white headed waves at home he loved the most. He opened his eyes and watched the rolls of water under the rapids, the water becoming the falls. He pushed himself to the surface, needing air and was pulled back down before he could rise. He tried again and ran out of air. The water held him under as Alex began to panic, wanting air. Unable to rise Alex knew he would drown, held tight in place by his rope. He wanted, needed to be free of it. Alex pulled at the rope, his good sailor's knot, his father teaching him well. It wouldn't undo.

Alex realized suddenly they must already think him dead. He'd been gone so long, they'd heard nothing. He saw them dredging the lake, walking the shore. All his cousins, his aunts and uncles, Fran and Reggie. Reggie who must be sicker than sick fishing without Alex, Alex the only one who could save him if he were ever to fall. They would have searched and given up. The light in the window gone, Alex forgotten by now, Reggie alone in their bed. Alex dead without his knowing. He was crying now, wanted home, was being pulled hard, feet first. He was unable to free himself and unable to rise, a breech birth death pulled to the edge of the falls.

A boy with so many brothers and sisters, never alone, always someone there, always someone waiting, watching for him.

But not this time.

AFTER THE LAWYERS HALL THEY WENT TO the Normal School. Colonel Gray of PEI gave a speech and then all the boys were given a holiday. One who waved to them looked just like Russell and Mercy felt a twinge of guilt. She hadn't written, did not have a gift yet for Russell or her younger sisters who were waiting and eager for them to come home again. All the delegates were there except for John A. The men shook hands with the boys and then left to return to the talks.

Mercy was left to gather with the women. She looked around her, could not quite believe this morning was done, after waiting all night, after the speeches and the rain, and she raised her hand to touch her hair.

She avoided her mother. Thought of John A. The promise of more, wanting away, fallen in love over the span of twelve hours, waiting for him to show.

They went to the museum. It was a large stone building with wide steps leading up to it. Only a museum, Mercy thought, yet it was bigger than Province House at home with only its threshold to step across. Inside it was dim, and Mercy stretched her arms, held back a yawn. She found it hard to pay attention to anything till they came to a room with a skylight and a pretend scene with birds and small animals in trees, butterflies suspended in the air. Blue sky and sun filtered through. There was a chance yet, a busy time now, all the talks. She'd see him yet; there was Niagara Falls yet, hoping.

She crossed her arms and ran her hands along them, felt the warmth of sun on her dress, the pressure of her hand on her arm. Wanting that touch, still wanting.

In the next room butterflies were pinned under glass, their wings translucent, veined like the petals of flowers. She wished she could feel them and reached out, ran her finger over the threads of colour beneath the glass. She read what she already knew, how if you touched a butterfly's wings you would disturb the dust on its hairs too fine to see, upset its balance so it couldn't fly, and it would die.

She traced a wing of blue, never having seen one like that before. Mercy always wanted to know the feel of everything. In her grandmother's back garden, the summer she was ten, a summer of butterflies, lighting on her arm, her hand. They'd quivered in a breeze too slight to feel, waited, while she reached out her hand and touched them. She couldn't help herself. Fearless or foolish, they stayed on her arm. A sixth sense of trust gone wrong, a failing of perception. When they ought to have known better, wanting that touch, believing, trusting, wanting more. Like her.

REGGIE WALKED ALONG THE EDGE OF SHORE and kept his eyes down. He did not want to see another fish, did not want to see anything but the sand beneath his feet. This the no man's land between water and the land. The sand where he walked now became sea or land at the whim of the sea, the wind, the moon. Careful, he walked only that ridge of sand but not careful enough. He was caught by a stray wave; the water splashed up on the leg of his pants. Reggie stopped and looked down, his feet and legs wet. He turned and looked out at the water, at the sea rolling in, the full moon tide of fall. Anything to be washed ashore coming ashore now, when the tide came in. Like the fish. He shuddered, unable to get the sight of it out of his mind.

Reggie turned and walked back along the line of collapsed sand. The waves ran in and he liked the cold numbness of his ankles, the sea at his feet. He was unable to walk away from it, knew he belonged to it, the sea written in his bones. Knew he would never, could never leave. He walked back to the fish, the water draining away so that the fish lay in a damp puddle the size of itself. Reggie stared at it, the texture of its skin a dull glisten in the morning light. It didn't move. He nudged towards it with his foot, its tail slowly flailing sand as the water seeped away. The fish was stranded, drowning in air. Like the fish in the hold of their boat, the gasp of their gills, and the sound of them against each other. Reggie knew the feel of them, their animalness as they squirmed and died. His stomach rolled. He turned away and was sick. He walked to the water and reached his hand down, wet his mouth, the salt of the water dry in his throat and mouth. He spat trying to get the taste of it away and couldn't. The salt dried on his lips, tasted like blood, like tears. Reggie walked back up to the fish. He watched it a moment, then took a breath and leaned down. He used both hands and picked it up.

The fish lay still. It was heavy like that, a big fish to be blown in, a good catch. It was awkward and difficult to hold away from his body. Dead, he thought, too late. He walked towards the water and the fish moved hard against him. Mustering its strength, it moved as though swimming in his hands and he nearly dropped it. Reggie held it more tightly, closer to his body and walked to the water's edge.

He stepped into the water, the waves rushing up at him as he held the fish. God, what was he thinking? Not thinking at all, just taking the fish back in. He would walk in and drop the fish out deeper where it wouldn't be blown back, where it could swim out away from the tide. The water seeped up his clothes and Reggie didn't notice the thrust of it against his shins as he walked in deeper. He was up to his waist and held the fish higher, not ready yet to let it go. He kept his eyes on the sea as the waves pushed in at him. Every wave in, half a wave pulled back out. Only a fish, what did he care? He didn't realize he was crying. And still he walked forward, the unfisherman.

Intent only on the fish now, Reggie felt it move, held it tighter. He was almost up to his chest. Then up to his shoulders, a whispered oh God. All for the saving of a foolish fish. The fish knowing the water below it, struggled against Reggie, fell from his hands. The water from its fall splashed up into Reggie's face and mouth. Startled and surprised, he stopped. In that moment of being startled, his attention let go, he loosened the hold on his body no longer holding the fish so tightly. In that short moment, a wave smaller than the others he'd stood against, took him, toppled him over and pushed him under. A surprised "oh" coming up in a bubble from his mouth.

THE NATURE OF WATER, MOVING, FOLLOWING ITS course, yielding to hard rock and wearing it away, rock becoming sand and rope too unable to hold, wearing down, breaking. The river flowing, took loose stones, unwary fish and stray boys, all loose and untied bodies pulled to the edge of the falls. The water pulling so hard, Alex's arms raised, an upside down dive, and he was freed of the rope. And there a fish trying to swim upstream, facing backwards like he was, caught in the breakwater of Alex's body. The fish held in Alex's arms as they fell together over the edge.

AFTER LUNCH MERCY AND HER MOTHER WENT to the Music Hall to hear the men. Only she and her mother went. In case, in case, still waiting, wanting to believe. The sun and the moon, hope loving hope. She looked behind her as they went in the door, as though she would find him there, waiting for her.

They listened to George Brown and a Red River man, Louis Riel. More land, more country, the great Northwest, the country expanding ever west. More great lakes and plains of grasses that spread across vast distances, waved in the wind like the sea, Riel said. Land as big as the sea Mercy thought. The sea become land and the land sea. Canada wanting more would make the sea land, join her island, and then the island a blood red puddle caught by the earth and rock and grass of the Canadas. The island and Mercy, both of them led astray, caught and held.

Canada wanting more. When it already had so much, and he wasn't there.

JOHN A HEAVY WITH SLEEP, ROLLED OVER and turned his face away from the afternoon sun that slanted in through the drawn curtains, the dim room lit by the sunny slant of light falling on the row of bottles looking gay and festive on the table.

REGGIE WAS CAUGHT IN THE SEA DRIFT, drowning as he knew he would, as his father wanted, as he was supposed to do. He was rocked in a lazy sea sway, the storm done, the tide a slow and easy pull in and out, and Reggie under the water, rising to the surface. An unexpected peace, a moment of reverie, Reggie let the sea take him. He opened his eyes with wonder as he floated staring up at the sky. On top of the water, floating, a salt water ease, Reggie slowly pushed in to shore.

November 4th. Niagara Falls

THE TRIP TO THE FALLS WAS TO be the final stop, everyone would turn around then, go home. Except for Mercy and her mother and father who were going on to relatives in Boston, Cleveland, Chicago, the trip of a lifetime. A lifetime. Mercy's stomach fell as they reached Hamilton and turned back on themselves, rounded the lake, headed back east, turned towards home. Everything was over and ended as though it had never happened. She would return home again and all was just the same. At the train all the delegates came to see them off, except for John A. She knew he wouldn't show. An islander, always an islander. And always the sea, stopping her. Hope deceived by hope.

ALL ALEX COULD SEE WAS WHITE. WHITE spray of water heavy like rain surrounded him as he fell. He took a gasp of air finally as he went over the edge, his stomach in a lurch like the boat as it rose on a wave and then was suddenly dropped, the wave interrupted. The force of the water against the weight of the two, fish and boy still together, pushed them out and away from the rocks as if they were wake. The coincidence of water and air, carried by both, away from the rocks.

Alex and the fish were submerged together. Both knew how to swim, but one wanted air. Drowning in water, deceived by water, by his own foolishness: longing for water as though it were home. Crying, he'd wanted it, wanted his brother. White waterfall of sky as he fell, and white sky of cloud overhead as he rose. Foolish and saved, miracle boy who survived the falls. Coincidence the opposite of faith.

MERCY AND HER FATHER STOOD UNDER TABLE Rock, the tunnels and window of rock behind the falls and it was just as John A had said. The water sprayed in at them, and she was soaked through, her gloves were wet and her hair even under her cape. She watched the gusts of water blown in at them, shifting patterns of white, like swallows, like snow caught in a storm.

"Home," her father said beside her watching the water as it fell, "I can't wait to get home again." The river here joined the lake and then the St. Lawrence, became salt water, reached their island, "Home is what I always wanted," a lovelorn loss in his voice.

Mercy turned away from him. She closed her eyes, heard only the sound of the water, felt the wet on her face. The one who was always left, left again. Her father turned to join the others writing their names in paint on the wall. All of them laughed as they saw their names. Mercy lingered behind, was the last to write her name on the rock wall, the beginning misting over even as she wrote the end. Their names foolish in paint, water wearing rock and paint away, insignificant against this fall of water. And yet there. For the time being, there.

AUTHOR'S NOTE

Sources that have been invaluable in the writing of this book include Mercy Coles' unpublished diary of the Quebec Conference in the National Archives of Canada, Christopher Moore's book, *1867: How the Fathers Made a Deal,* Shane Peacock's book, *The Great Farini,* and the Prince Edward Island newspapers of the time from the Provincial Archives in Charlottetown.

Photo by Don Hall

ANNE MCDONALD has been writing for sixteen years and her work has appeared in *The Society* and *Descant* and has been broadcast on CBC Radio. *The Coincidence of Water and Air* (original title of *To the Edge of the Sea*) was First Alternate for the John V. Hicks fiction manuscript award in 2010.